The Treehouse

To Bobbie,

Thank you for purchasing my novel. I truly hope you enjoy all three stories. You are a wonderful student and I expect great things from you. If you ever need anything, please do not hesitate to call.

Mr. Bruno

The Treehouse

Al Bruno

Library of Congress Control Number:		2011905084
ISBN:	Hardcover	978-1-4568-9649-2
	Softcover	978-1-4568-9648-5
	Ebook	978-1-4568-9650-8

To order additional copies of this book, contact:
Xlibris Corporation
1-888-795-4274
www.Xlibris.com
Orders@Xlibris.com
95119

DEDICATED TO:

My Mother, Candida . . .
My Father (R.I.P.) Jesus . . .
Yolanda and Nicholas, the inspiration for my life . . .
Miriam, Ivelesse, Sara, and Ferdinand . . .
John, Frank, Carlos, Christopher, Jason, Albert, and Michael . . .
My surrogate English moms: Ellen Scheinbach, Anne Piotrowski,
and Karen Andronico . . .
Chris Drew, my sinister acquaintance of the macabre . . .
"The Fellas": Frankie, Carlos, and Oscar . . .
Mike Casey, Gary Gli, Relson Gracie, Wilfredo, Ishmael, John,
Steve, Adam, Butch, and all of the members
of the Relson Gracie Jiu Jitsu Academy in the Bronx . . .
Shinan Hector Negron, Sensei Reggie, Sensei Chris Donovan,
Sensei Jacob, Sensei Phil, Sensei Garcia, and all of the members
of the San Yama Bushi Judo Club in New Rochelle, New York . . .
and finally my esteemed colleagues at M.S. 118 and Herbert H. Lehman H.S.
All of these wonderful people have contributed to this book
by allowing me to be a part of their lives.

CONTENTS

SAVING A NATION

SAVING A NATION

There smites nothing so sharp, nor smelleth so sour as shame.
—William Langland, *Piers Plowman*

S EVERAL SLICES OF wheat bread made their way out of the opened plastic bag on the counter. A butter knife lay draped across the top of the half-full container of margarine that pressed against the salt and pepper shakers; a second knife was submerged in a large jar of light mayonnaise. Two cellophane wrappers—one exposing a small mountain of peppercorn turkey that released the tender smell of spice, the other of Swiss cheese—were beside a pitcher of home-made orange juice. A bowl of cereal with thin slices of bananas floating on top, like tiny lifesavers, and granulated flaxseeds and an empty glass were just opposite the loaf of bread. Next to the juice were two sixteen-ounce cans on top of a blue plastic bag, the receipt pinned underneath one of the cans. Several unopened letters peeked out from underneath the toaster.

"Is this it?" Kathryn held one of the sixteen-ounce cans of cherrywood stain at eye level. "How long does it take to dry?"

Chuck took a bite of his sandwich, nodded, and reached for his water.

"It says here that you have to allow the stain to penetrate the wood anywhere from five to fifteen minutes." She traced her index finger along the writing on the back label. "To achieve a darker color, a second coat can be applied four to six hours after the first one."

Chuck took another bite and nodded again. Kathryn placed the can on the table and walked to the fridge, opened the door, took out a gallon of pomegranate juice, and reached for the glass.

The last piece of sandwich disappeared into Chuck's mouth. He licked his fingers and swiped crumbs from his chest.

"When are you going to start?"

Chuck tapped the table with his index finger as he chugged the water. "Right now." He pushed himself away from the table and let out a loud burp.

"Excuse me." She shook her head.

"You're excused," he said over his shoulder and walked away.

"Hey! Picasso." She grabbed the can of wood stain and followed him. "Aren't you forgetting something?"

Chuck entered the garage and took out the lawnmower, a couple of plastic storage bins, and Kathryn's bike in order to gain access to the Victorian dresser they had picked up at a used-furniture store over a week ago. Although he wasn't much of an antique connoisseur, he had to admit that the dresser was indeed quite remarkable. Kathryn had been hinting at wanting a new dresser for the guest room for quite some time. They had visited numerous department stores and compared prices, but when the price tag of the cheapest dresser was a hefty $450, they opted to visit a used-furniture store where she found *her* dresser. Kathy wasted no time in running down a list of other items needed to compliment their new purchase during the drive home.

"It's only the guest room," Chuck had remarked.

"Yeah, but it needs to match the bed," she responded.

"Nobody ever stays with us."

"My mother."

"Oh yeah, that's right." He tightened his grip on the steering wheel and smiled.

The legs on the solid oak dresser began to cry as they scraped the concrete floor. Chuck stopped and knelt to survey the damage and shot a glance over his shoulder.

"Shit." *If Kathy sees this, she'll have a fit.* He got up and went to the other side of the garage, shoved aside a couple of boxes, and found the dolly. He placed it on the floor and pushed it with his leg. The wheels squealed louder than the dresser; one of the wheels was seized and left a black line on the floor. He reached over the bicycle for a can of WD-40 lubricant on the shelf and sprayed the wheels. After about five minutes, half a can of lubricant, and several trial runs of pushing the dolly across the floor in zigzag patterns, he picked it up and loaded the dresser sideways onto the dolly and out to the driveway. Kathy wanted the dresser stained cherry-red to match the bed and night table in the guestroom. This dresser was oak and had apparently given testimony to a couple of generations. Nonetheless, it had been kept in pretty good condition. And, as Kathy had commented, the furniture back then was made out of "real wood" by "real artisans." He had to agree. Nowadays, everything was practically made out of compressed chips of wood glued together with some sort of resin; and once humidity got a hold of it, the wood would boomerang into all sorts of shapes. If you wanted a "real" dresser out of "real" wood, you'd have to spend a paycheck and a half. The more he thought about it, this $125 dresser and the cans of wood stain and polyurethane coating for under $25 was indeed a bargain. All he had to do was sand, stain, and paint.

"Okay, let's get to work." He grabbed several sheets of 60, 100, and 220 grit sandpaper from a shelf. He patted the top of the dresser. "Time for your facelift."

He began at the top with the 60-grit sandpaper to remove larger pieces of flaked stain: the 40-grit would remove them much better, but at the expense of chipping the surface. A cloud of dust shrouded the dresser and settled in his hair, face, and clothes. The sweat on his arms trapped dust to create minute pools of mud. He sneezed a couple of times and took a break to allow the dust to disappear.

Half an hour later, Kathy emerged from the garage with two cans of beer.

"You read my mind." He let the sandpaper fall to the floor, wiped his palms on his pants, and reached for the beer. "Thanks." A small geyser shot from the opening as he pulled back on the tab and raised the can to his mouth. "Ahhh!" He ran a forearm across his forehead and left behind lanes of caked dirt.

"Wow!" Kathy smiled as she ran her palm across the top. "It's still a bit rough though."

Chuck waved at the dresser as if swatting away smoke. "Just getting the old paint off. I have to smooth it out later on."

"Can't wait to see it." She tapped the dresser and left.

"Get me another beer!"

Chuck sat in his driveway with a mountain of sandpapers surrounding him. He watched the sun as it laid to rest behind the clouds. The last traces of daylight danced across the horizon in hues of oranges, yellows, and red. Engulfing these colors were different shades of blues and purples with the darkness of night gradually ascending to assume control of its shift. He took a deep breath, raised himself from the floor, looked at the dresser, checked his watch and decided to call it a day. Tomorrow, he would get started on the drawers. He began to remove the drawers: there were eight in all. Once removed, the dresser was easier to place on the dolly. He pushed it into the garage.

The sun had been swallowed by the horizon. Chuck grabbed two drawers at a time and brought them in. He yawned and picked up the last two drawers, sneezed, and dropped one of them.

"Damn." He picked up the drawer, and a small dusty leather-bound book fell out. "What in the—?" Chuck placed both drawers on the floor and picked up the book. He walked to the entrance of the garage while flipping through the pages: it appeared to be a diary. He brushed some of the dirt from the cover and turned to the opening page to reveal the name "William" beautifully written in script from a quill pen: the last two words had all but disappeared. The following page had a phrase written in the center: *Forgive me, Lord, for my lack of courage.* He thumbed through the book. There was a newspaper clipping neatly tucked in between the pages. Chuck pulled it out carefully and placed the diary on the dresser to unfold the clipping and scanned the headlines:

NEW YORK HERALD

FINAL EDITION—NEW YORK—TUESDAY, APRIL 16, 1912

OVER 1,500 DIE AS THE GREAT TITANIC FLOUNDERS

Chuck's hands trembled like the time he found his Christmas gift tucked away in between two bedsheets in the laundry room while looking for a clean towel. After that, he would peek at it every day before finally opening it eight days later. He never told his mother.

He placed the clipping on top of the dresser, ran inside to get a beer, and barged into the garage, knocking over Kathy's bicycle, nearly tripping over it. He dragged a chair, sat on the edge, and took a deep breath. Some of the opening pages crumbled at the edges as he turned them. Chuck pictured himself carefully tearing the wrapping paper as he opened the box that had the walkie-talkies he had asked Santa for a couple of decades ago. He took several gulps of beer and stopped at the first page.

April 14, 1913
"Wow." He leaned back and began to read.

I have finally summoned the courage to write about that fateful night.

April 14, 1912. That night will forever haunt me. I still shiver at the events that took place on that cold evening. Every time I close my eyes, I see them: they are there. Two of them rushing toward the boat, parallel to each other; Poseidon's fingers skirting underneath the waves, leaving behind a trail of displaced water as they neared the luxurious liner on her maiden voyage. The soft whooshing of miniature propellers: a silent death. Sure, believe what you may in the tabloids, but were you to ask me in private, I would unveil the truth. The iceberg story was credible and has been etched in stone. I could not, dared not, refute it. I was merely acting out of the interest and safety of an entire nation. Though my predecessor would have been vehemently opposed to my somewhat inglorious approach to running the country, it was my duty to keep America exempt from global conflict. And although history may document otherwise, it was no accident. An iceberg did not sink the *Titanic*.

I was returning home incognito from a very much-deserved two-week vacation in Italy; I have always been fascinated with ancient Rome. Only the captain and a selected group of officers knew about my staff members and me. I had been scheduled to throw out the ceremonial first pitch at Griffith Stadium in 1912, but my esteemed colleague, Sherman, was bestowed with the honor by the Washington Senators. The papers had stated that I had missed the opportunity to throw out the ceremonial first pitch because I was attending the funeral of my beloved friend, Archie. If they had only known the truth. He was at my side on that infamous night. Oh, Archie, my friend! You will forever be missed.

The grandeur of Rome erased this homesickness. I submerged myself in extensive, and often exhaustive, sightseeing. I had purposely reserved the Coliseum for last. It is here that I paused to catch my breath and rest my aching feet. I detached myself from the group, took a seat, closed my eyes, and listened to the voices of souls long gone: the maniacal litany of the frenzied masses as they cheered the gladiators, the clanging of metal against metal, the roaring of beasts, all culminating in agonizing death throes. A sudden breeze jarred my reverie. I opened my eyes and sighed heavily, took off my glasses, and pressed my fingers on the bridge of my nose. It was impossible to believe how such an elegant structure had given testimony to such barbarous acts. Such beauty that man is capable of. And now, as my thoughts return to the present, what atrocities are men also capable of inflicting. That is why I opted to concur with the events of that night. Having sensed the growing animosity on European soil, especially after the dismissal of that honorable gentleman Otto von Bismarck, I was reluctant to lead this nation into further conflict. Four decades ago, we were involved in a war that divided the nation: the wounds have yet to heal. Had I known that we would inevitably be sucked into this maelstrom of chaos a couple of years later under the supervision of my Democratic successor, I would have stated to the press with certainty and honesty what I witnessed that evening as I gazed upon the luminous orb bursting through the celestial veil in the warm, frigid air . . .

I smiled as thoughts of home swam around my mind like dreams submerged in the ocean. Every breath of air I expelled was manifested in small mists. My ears tingled and droplets of dew froze on my mustache. But inside me, there was a feeling of warmth one gets when sitting around the fireplace in a cozy cottage as the snow gently falls outside. I looked upon the horizon, watching as the distant icebergs courted each other in silence. They resembled families of monolithic snow cones. We were approaching one of these icy behemoths; it was then when I spotted the ebony silhouette. There was a brief flash of light as it moved from right to left. Minutes later, it was at our side about five hundred yards out. About a dozen or so passengers were scattered about the deck, but none were in range to witness what I was seeing. *A whale?* And just as the question popped into my head, it was quickly answered by the constant linear trajectory of the object. There were no interrupted crescentlike swimming patterns of whales, nor was there the whooshing of air of a Leviathan surfacing. This "thing" continued on a straight, undeterred path. The object from which these two entities had been expelled diminished in size as it disappeared into the icy abyss. Meanwhile, the parent iceberg drew nearer. Moments later, the devil's horns were pointing at the ship, gaining ground and closing the distance between them and the hull of the ship.

Torpedoes!

The navy had informed me of the recent U-boat operations in the Atlantic: I should have paid more attention to their reports. It was during this time that the Germans had taken to the sea. They had adopted a policy of unrestricted submarine warfare, which declared that all ships, regardless of if they were commercial or civilian passenger ships, were to be treated as military targets and could therefore be fired upon should they somehow find their way into disputed waters. This aggressive policy of mare nostrum placed us on high alert, not to mention the extreme threat it posed to the rest of Europe, especially the United Kingdom, which was practically under siege by this abhorrent naval tactic adopted by Germany. But, though the threat was great, it was still my responsibility as captain of this nation to steer America away from tumultuous waters. In the end, it did not work. This illustrious vessel proved to be one of Germany's first successful trial runs. The second, which was more overt, took place on May 7, 1915. By then the Western world was given a more crude and horrific display of their U-boat capabilities. Had I known they were to claim 1,198 more lives aboard the *Lusitania*, I would disclose the horrors of that evening.

As I stepped back from the rail and braced myself against a deck pole for the impact, I heard the frantic clanging of bells as the men in the crow's nest yelled, "Iceberg! Iceberg right ahead!" I turned and looked on as my soul pounded away from inside like a blacksmith in an attempt to break free through my chest as the iceberg grew in size. I took two steps away from the pole, unable to take a third. And just as the ship hastened to greet the ivory mountain, there came thunder and lightning. An orange ball of flame shot up the side of the hull to where I had been standing just moments ago then disappeared just as quickly. A fraction of a second later, the liner embraced the iceberg. I later discovered that the explosion other passengers claimed to have seen—as I had—had been attributed to the damage caused to the boilers and engine room, a very plausible explanation.

The liner danced with the iceberg for about ten seconds. I felt myself floating until my body slammed against metal, shielding myself from the chunks of ice that slammed onto the deck and slumped to the ground. The vibrations from the impact shook every cell in my body. I crawled about like a drunkard trying to get up to no avail. Suddenly, I was being pulled off the floor like a newborn. It was the master-at-arms. "Are you okay?" he asked. I nodded. He ran to the rails, leaned over, and began surveying the damage. By now, the deck was swamped with officers and more passengers: some clad in tuxedos, others in sleepwear. I could hear First Officer Murdoch barking orders at several of the men from "Get down to the engine room and assess the damage" to "Inform the passengers to remain calm. There is absolutely no reason to panic."

Minutes after the collision, I began to regain my faculties and was able to walk with greater composure. Just then, Captain Smith appeared. His suspenders hung from an unbuttoned jacket and one-half of his shirt untucked. The crowd of officers parted as he made his way to Murdoch, who pointed at the iceberg that had caused the damage—or so it would be chronicled as such in history—as it disappeared into the night. Once they had finished talking, the captain pulled him to the side, whispered some orders, and sent him on his way. Captain Smith took a couple of steps, stopped, and stared into the icy, ebony horizon.

"Captain," I half yelled. He gazed at me for a second or two, blinked, and then acknowledged me. "Captain Smith. I . . ." *I saw what caused the damage. I know what happened.* But the words would not come out. *It's not our war!* my mind screamed.

"Mr. President," he grinned and stared at my forehead. "You're bleeding."

I touched my forehead gingerly: there was blood on my fingers. "Yes, I see. Well, there are other matters that require more attention." I nodded in the direction of the damage.

He turned his head mechanically toward the men leaning over the rail as they pointed to the damage below. Just then, Officer Murdoch and Mr. Thomas Andrews—a director of Harland and Wolff, the company that had built the ill-fated liner—approached us at a trot. The captain excused himself as the maritime triumvirate disappeared into the bowels of the ship. I rubbed my hands vigorously and touched my forehead once again: the blood had almost congealed. Around me, a controlled pandemonium. Men scurried from one end of the ship to the other. Passengers gathered in groups. A circle of men clad in penurious attire—weathered jackets, untidy pants, and unkempt boots—kicked a chuck of ice back and forth. A couple of them clanked their mugs of ale and laughed. Some leaned over the rails and gasped while others snickered in defiance as they claimed the vessel to be unsinkable. "A couple of hours at most. We'll be moving in no time," I heard a man say as he took a sip of brandy. "You'll see there's nothing to worry about." He stomped the deck. "Solid as the Rock of Gibraltar." I shook my head in disbelief and turned to see the captain standing by himself. He closed his eyes and leaned his head slightly back. I approached him.

"Captain, is there something wrong?" His silence revealed the answer. I sighed. "How much time do we have?"

"Mr. President, you need to come with me." He forced a smile. Mr. Ismay was pacing outside his cabin. Captain Smith escorted Ismay and

I into his cabin and spun a tale of terror as he passed around the bottle of brandy. The frigid hands of the sea had crawled into numbers 1, 2, 3, and 6 boiler rooms and penetrated into number 5 as well, sending hundreds of men to unspeakable deaths amid a combination of burning coal and subzero waters. I pressed my fingers against my lips to keep the liquor in. Moments later, I was escorted to my room by one of his senior officers to gather up blankets and other personal belongings.

I must note that although the captain had allocated a room in first class for Archie and me, along with a couple of friends, my initial request was a room in second class. The rooms were furnished quite elegantly, and the passengers consisted of a good, decent lot of merchants and self-employed men. The accommodations in first class were exquisite, but I felt a tad queer around the passengers whose overall demeanor was comprised of vanity, charades, and foolishness all neatly tucked into a façade of subtle arrogance. Archie and I enjoyed but two meals among the elitists, deciding not to indulge in a third. Thereafter, we either had our food delivered, prepared it ourselves (we had our own kitchen, and Archie was quite handy on the stove), or picked from the buffet and stealthily made our way to our quarters amid several glances of disapproval. We ate our meals on the veranda overlooking the sea, engaging in conversation and sharing humor. The view was spectacular, especially at sunset. The privacy allowed me to indulge myself in books from the library aboard the *Titanic*. Archie, on the other hand, enjoyed visits to the gymnasium and the racquetball court, which I once attempted at the expense of near heart failure.

I exited the room and paused momentarily to look at the two suitcases in my hands.

"Mr. President, we must get going." The senior officer looked at me. "Would you like me to carry one of those for you, Mr. President?" He already had a suitcase in hand and reached for another.

"No." I sighed. "The space will be needed." We returned the suitcases to the room. I grabbed more blankets. "These will serve us better."

"Yes, Mr. President." He smiled and nodded approvingly. "They will."

We made a couple of stops to gather up my staff. I gave them the condensed version of what had transpired. Some closed their eyes while others asked, "What are we going to do?" to which I replied, "We're doing it right now."

We reached the deck. I stopped. Could it be? Were my ears deceiving me, or was that "In the Shadows" that I was listening to? I cocked my head to see one of the bravest, or foolish, acts of mankind. Mr. Wallace Hartley and his band were engaged in a *concerto finale*. The music had a calming effect, and I was momentarily compelled to pay tribute, but Archie interrupted my solace nearly ripping my arm at its shoulder. "We must go!" he almost shouted. I nodded. The senior officer quickly led us to a lifeboat and handed us lifejackets. Some of the people on board welcomed us, others just stared. Some were clad in tuxedos and topcoats while others had been pulled from their beds and covered themselves in blankets. I found a seat. There were two women and a man who fixed their eyes on me. One of the women leaned over and whispered into the other woman's ear, who in turn whispered into the man's ear. They smiled curtly. The man leaned over and shook my hand. "It's a pleasure to meet you," he whispered. I returned the handshake and thanked them in silence for their discretion. Several others had boarded the lifeboat, and about ten minutes later, we were being lowered into the water. I took a quick headcount—twenty-three: thirteen women, six children, and four men, not including a steward, two hands, and two boatswains. There was room for plenty more bodies, at least twenty more. It is here that my pen quivers as I hang my head in guilt and melancholy. As is always obvious in life, everything can be remedied *after* the events have occurred. The case with the lifeboats was no different and perhaps among the most troublesome: they had been designed to carry a minimum of sixty people. *Hundreds of more lives could have been saved!* But the extreme vanity that was displayed amid the chaos had reaffirmed the societal pecking order that designated first-class passengers as the chosen lot. Even now at sea, during a time in which the jaws of the ocean were slowly devouring steel and flesh, when hundreds of lives were at stake—women, children, men—even now we could not escape Darwinist doctrines. In the end, third class had been sacrificed to save the elite. The Egyptians, Greeks, Romans—had we not learned the value of life? Did we ever truly progress?

The lifeboat swung like a pendulum as it descended. The people huddled together like oxen. There was a small explosion followed by a flash of light that traced its way upward. A mixture of gasps and screams filled the night. Once it had reached its apex, there was a second

AL BRUNO

explosion that lit up the sky like a white umbrella. More screaming. I shielded my eyes as shadows danced a dance macabre. Some of the women yelled to their husbands above. Some cursed and complained, promising to sue the White Star Line for every penny once they set foot ashore. Some sobbed silently while others had to be restrained. The rest stared vacantly into the dark, icy waters that lay ahead. A woman hugged her child. *There, there.* And as the lifeboat distanced itself from Charon's ferry, our breaths became more highlighted. The night had not finished with us; it was merely preparing us for act 2: those who were not to be claimed by the sea were left to brave subzero temperatures amid the grim, unholy solitude that can only be found at sea. The warmth that had been produced by the rush of adrenaline amid the hour of evacuation had been replaced by the presentiment of death. As I sat shivering, I wondered which of the two was worse: perishing amid glacial waters or suffering a slow Siberian death in the Atlantic.

Pardon me, I have lost track of time. The time of occurrence is now the eve of April 15. Our nightmare has spilled onto the next day . . .

I caught a glimpse of the captain as he leaned on the rail above. Another flare was launched. He scanned the lifeboat until he found me. I wanted to wave goodbye, but fear had glued my arms to my sides. He saluted while I managed half a salute. The descending light cast a shadow on the captain: there stood a corpse in his place. The lifeboat bumped against the side of the *Titanic.* I nearly fell backward and grabbed onto an oarlock. Somebody screamed. "Hey! Watch it, you moron," a man yelled. One of the women held a rosary. Her lips trembled either from the horror or the cold or both as she recited a prayer for all of us, or perhaps just herself. When I looked up, the captain was gone.

We reached the water. One of the seamen undid the ropes and grabbed the oars while another lit a lantern. As we began to distance ourselves from the liner, I could see hundreds of people running frantically back and forth on the bridge deck. Two more flares fled the *Titanic* simultaneously; seconds later, two more. A serene chaos interrupted the maelstrom unfolding as the quartet of flares huddled together like mushrooms in the sky. There was crying, shouting, and cursing. I could see seamen, who were outnumbered by a staggering amount, struggling to keep mobs from lifeboats. They pushed against the motley crews with oars, only to have them snatched and used against them. Some of the seamen were swallowed by the crowd. By this time, anarchy and bedlam had gained control. Several lifeboats had managed to escape. Suddenly, the sound of twisting metal charged into the scene. A blanket of silence enveloped the crowd. The running subsided. Smokestacks bent, snapped, and crashed on the deck of the doomed vessel and into the water, crushing hundreds of screaming souls. *Their hell is over. Ours has just begun.*

"Dear Lord," the man next to me whispered. He uncorked a bottle of VSOP Cognac with his teeth, spat the cork over the side, bent his elbow, and began to empty the bottle. Tears streamed down the women's faces. The rowing stopped. One of the seamen stared in silence with mouth agape. Another woman buried her face in her hands. I closed my eyes and prayed with the woman.

Poseidon's blood poured into the iron sarcophagus. I prayed for the stokers below whose last glimpse of daylight was when they boarded the *Titanic*. Because of their location, which was below the waterline, Fate had paid them the first visit.

I had been given a tour of the boiler rooms by First Officer Murdoch two days before. The sight was quite appalling. Soot-covered men fed coal into the insatiable cavernous boilers. I could not distinguish one man from the other. Some simply ignored me while others tipped their hats. Were it not for Archie, I would have tasted some coal after tripping over a small pile near boiler number 3. Breathing became a chore. Blasts of heat catapulted themselves at me, and with every breath that I took, my lungs felt like two hot bellows. I informed Officer Murdoch that I had seen enough for the day.

The last two flares painted their way upward like white embers and burst into the final hope for the hundreds that had been sentenced. The bow of the ship angled itself perpendicular amid the illumination. Dozens upon dozens of desperate souls fell like confetti from the ship. I could watch no more. I squeezed my eyes shut and prayed harder and louder amid the screams of the women, the cursing of men, the crying of children, and the dreadful noise as the sea's tongue reached deeper into the ship, forcing out windows in small explosions. And beneath it all, the choir of hundreds of perishing souls coming together as one. I turned in time to catch a final glimpse of the stern and propellers as they were swallowed up by the sea. A couple of lifeboats were drawn backward and disappeared into the churning funnel. A muffled splash sealed the jaws of the ocean as Poseidon cleared his throat, leaving behind a trail of debris and orphaned passengers as the only clues of the earthly existence of the *Titanic*. In less than three hours, the waters off the south of the Grand Banks of Newfoundland had claimed the *Titanic*.

The *Californian*, as I was later told, had been in the area during those fateful hours. Countless lives, if not all, could have been saved. Yet, as I look back, the large ice field that had forced Captain Lord to stop the ship and wait until the morning was divine intervention; for had they come to our aide, their fate could have been the same as ours.

(It must be noted that several crew members from the *Californian* witnessed another ship in that area as I had when the *Titanic* sunk. This "phantom ship theory" that the crew and captain swore by yet whose identity has never been revealed has been the subject of grave controversy. And judging from the incessant slandering and finger-pointing at the crew of the *Californian*, it will continue to serve as fodder for the tabloids and pointless conversations. Oh, how I longed for the courage to swear by Captain Lord's account and remove the mask of the offender!)

I must mention, for it is not only proper but necessary to honor bravery, dedication, and extreme altruism in sacrificing one's own life for another that these pages would not have been written had I not had my venerable and honorable friend, Maj. Archibald Butt, at my side. While boarding the lifeboat, I waved the major in and patted the empty space beside me, but he smiled and escorted a mother and her child aboard. I grabbed the boy and sat him beside me and comforted him as best as I could. Archie handed me his dinner jacket. "Keep the lad warm, Willie." We stared at one another. He smiled. Never before and never after that did I experience such admiration for a man. That was the last time I saw him.

I cannot tell with certitude how long Hades toyed with us, for my thoughts were as numb as my body. The crying had diminished, as did the chattering. The stomping of feet had lessened. Puffs from coughing and breathing are all that remained as signs of life. I felt myself drifting like the patches of ice that surrounded us. I dared not move, could not move, for fear of spreading the cold throughout my body. I felt my body begin to relax as my mind swam in pools of memories of Mount Auburn . . .

I could smell the oatmeal cookies Mrs. Thatcher, our neighbor, used to give us on our way to school. *Gonna miss your cookies if you don't hurry*, Mama would say whenever she had problems getting us out of bed. Mr. Willoughby, the grumpy old fart who sat in his dilapidated rocking chair with a bottle of liquor and Lucky, a gnarly-haired mongrel that had lost an ear one day while old Willoughby decided to clean his shotgun after tilting the bottle all day. That old fleabag came off the porch with his tail tucked firmly between his legs yelping like Ol' Scratch was at his heels. Me and Timmy Doyle, whose sister I secretly admired, nearly peed our pants flying kites with Charles, Horace, and Henry. Charles always made the best kites: I learned from him. The time we ditched school to fly our newly made kites. Had it not been for Horace's scrapes on his arms and legs after he attempted to rescue the imprisoned kite from a tree, Mama would have never found out. Lying was a sin, especially in our house. And then there was the Philippines. How I loved to watch Robert, Charlie, and Helen run around in the backyard. My children, your father loves you very much! Nellie, my love. If I were but in your arms at this very moment. The warmth of your body would erase this cold hell. If I could but lose myself in your eyes, in your smile, my hands caressing your soft skin, the beating of your heart . . . Images of ballparks and golf courses became blurry. The people sitting across from me became one dark mass. It was then that the lights appeared on the horizon.

As the iron seahorse drew near, the letters RMS *Titanic* appeared. We were safe! There was absolutely nothing to worry about. I was finally awakening from this dreadful nightmare.

A young man extended his hand. I reached out and thanked him as he helped me to my feet. "It's good to be back aboard. That was some drill. Perhaps now we can get to New York without any further delays."

"Sir?" The seaman stopped. "Pardon me, sir, but this is the RMS *Carpathia*."

I looked over my shoulder, out to sea . . . "But of course," I responded as he led me to the steps.

I have finally reached the end of my endeavor. My thoughts are now concrete. *Who is my audience?* I myself am my audience. Yet I feel no peace. How foolish of me at conjuring fragile hopes of absolution within these pages. Someone once suggested that writing down one's problems is a most effective method to deal with one's fears, a method for confronting demons and conquering them with the stroke of a quill: the greatest of all fallacies! There is no comfort rather a grim remembrance of tragedy.

There will never be absolution; there will never be closure, nor will the final chapter on man's vanity ever be written. I cannot arrive at a rational, humane decision as to which of the two was worse: the sinking of the *Titanic* or the senseless lawsuits during the aftermath. My hands tremble with rage as the newspaper shook in my hands: 12 million dollars for diamonds, hundreds of thousands of dollars for necklaces, $3,000 for a photo signed by Garibaldi, bagpipes, dresses, prized books, reading glasses, and a myriad of other ludicrous claims. Even the bodies that were still being discovered a month after the sinking could not top these headlines. Is life less precious than a stone, a picture, or a musical instrument? I threw the newspaper aside and did not read another.

If there ever was a tale of foretold fate, then the short-lived saga of the *Titanic* is such a tale. William Thomas Stead's two earlier publications supported such a theory by providing an eerie premonition that followed him onto the deck of the *Titanic*. The first, in March of 1886, "How the Mail Steamer Went Down in Mid-Atlantic, by a Survivor," tells the harrowing accounts of a steamer that collides with another ship resulting in many deaths due to a lack of lifeboats. Ironically, Stead had gone on to claim that "this is exactly what might take place and will take place if liners are sent to sea short of boats." The second, and perhaps more ominous of the two, came in 1892. He published *From the Old World to the New*, a fictional story of a White Star Line vessel—the *Majestic*—that rescues survivors of another ship that collided with an iceberg; the captain's name is Edward Smith. Furthermore, on the very day of departure, the *Titanic* nearly collided with an American line vessel named *New York*. Stead was Fate's Lieutenant and Percy Shelley all in one. Was he the architect of disaster by way of his pen, or had *Titanic*'s script been written a millennium ago? Be that as it may, no force on this planet could have prevented the tragic outcome. Likewise, the final chapter in Stead's life had been written aboard the *Titanic*.

Some may deem my actions as both cowardly and unpatriotic, but I disagree. Better to have a thousand drown than one million perish in the battlefields had I decided to tell the truth. The lives of those on board, to include my colleagues Benjamin Guggenheim, John Jacob

Astor, and Isidor Straus, the latter with whom I had had the pleasure of enjoying a meal with earlier that evening, were expendable. The lives of millions of American soldiers were not.

End of entry.

William H. Taft

The letter felt like lead in Chuck's hands. He squeezed his eyes shut, forcing out a lonely tear. It scurried down his cheek and hung on his chin for a fraction of a second before leaping onto his shirt where it disappeared, leaving a small patch of wetness. Chuck pulled his T-shirt to dry his eyes. He sat up, placed the diary on the floor, and reached for his beer; it was empty. He leaned back and began to stare at the stars as if he had just discovered them. They stared back in perfect tranquility, projecting themselves from millions of miles away, from other universes, illuminating the night without words. These same stars that had been around for billions of years and had given testimony to Earth's history, from the age of the dinosaurs, the rise and fall of the Roman Empire, to the very acts of mankind that were currently taking place; even now as he sat back exchanging glances with them, his history was being recorded. And it was the stars that were the lone celestial audience to the tragedy of the *Titanic. Were these the same stars present during the sinking? The very same stars that the victims gazed upon during that fateful night?* And then a peculiar thought raced across his mind as he imagined the souls of the passengers passing in review before him amid the bluish blackness of the sky. Had they been reading along? If so, then the truth had been brought to light. Their souls could now rest in peace as the final chapter to their long-awaited rest had been read.

Chuck picked up the diary and stretched. There was definitely a story here. This was treasure. Television interviews, his name and story in print, and a host of public appearances, perhaps even a book deal. The money earned from rights and royalties would definitely come in handy. He smiled as a list of things he could do with the cash appeared in his mind.

He took a step into the garage and stopped, turned around, and looked up at the sky. The diary weighed down on his conscience like a press.

Would it be worth the money to stain the memory of a man who served his country during such a trying time? And what about the souls that still remained buried at the bottom of the Atlantic? Had they not endured enough grief?

The journal revealed the tortured thoughts of a man who had carefully hidden them in the last drawer. Had he hoped that some other generation would find this journal, read it, understand his position, and acquit him of this self-induced crime? The verdict was Chuck's.

He sauntered out into the middle of the driveway and held his hands in prayer with the journal clasped tightly between them, closed his eyes, and looked up.

"I understand you, Mr. President," he sighed. "You did the right thing." He took a deep breath. "You are free to rest in peace."

A cool, chilly, gentle wave of ocean breeze engulfed him, causing him to shiver slightly. The smell and taste of saltwater invaded his nostrils and palate, and the stars seemed to shine brighter. And just as it had appeared, the breeze subsided, and the stars dimmed.

BLUE SWEAT, WHITE BREEZE

BLUE SWEAT, WHITE BREEZE

In the sweat of thy face shalt thou eat bread.
—Old Testament, Genesis 3:19

THE FIERCE SUN had beamed down on the inhabitants of New York City for over a week, scorching them like sausages in an oven. Record-breaking temperatures of over 100 degrees Fahrenheit cooked people inside out for four consecutive days. Many laborers walked around shirtless while office workers worked without T-shirts, with sleeves rolled up and ties loosened. Many women paraded the streets braless with miniskirts made out of the thinnest fabric, occasionally slowing down traffic, evoking sexual innuendos reserved mainly for strip clubs. Children danced in front of open fire hydrants while fire marshals patrolled the city closing them down to keep water pressure from dropping; over a dozen people had died in a fire a day ago because of insufficient water pressure. Dogs lapped at every available puddle of water, panting and joining the kids in their watery festivities. Pigeons remained perched on tree limbs and shaded rooftops conserving their energy.

Power outages all over the city prompted the mayor to caution homeowners and businesses to please use air conditioners in extreme moderation. Rather than have three running at once in three different rooms, he suggested families congregate in two rooms to eliminate the usage of at least one unit. Con Edison had informed him that if everybody followed this formula, consumption of electricity could be cut down by two-fifths. Unfortunately, the majority opted for fully air-conditioned homes. Thus the outages had increased to about two a day, sometimes three. As a result, not only were telephone lines flooded with complaints, but supermarkets and delicatessens lost hundreds of thousands of dollars in merchandise while portable generator sales skyrocketed.

The interior of cars became pregnant with heat, suffocating passengers. Air-conditioned taxis became a highly valued commodity, and the cabs void of this luxury waited for hours at automotive repair shops to have their systems serviced. Likewise, every major appliance store in the city enjoyed an increase in sales on air conditioners. The people who could not afford them resorted to fans, which only transferred the hot, dry air from the outside into their homes.

Tempers flared. Crime rates ballooned. Those who had personal grievances in life experienced a deeper, more intrinsic rage with the heat. Road-rage incidents by angry, sweaty drivers in steamy, sweat-filled vehicles mushroomed. The honk of a horn would send drivers into a frenzy of cursing that occasionally turned into a punching mania, sending many back to their vehicles with the salty taste of blood in their mouths and others to emergency rooms.

Jacinto

By 7:45 a.m., the temperature had already reached sixty-five degrees Fahrenheit with the promise of at least another thirty added to that by midday. The warmth of the sun reached out just enough to provide comfort, and if only ten degrees were piled on top of the current temperature, the day would have been ideal. But the sun had other plans of its own, teasing with mild warmth in the morning before turning the knob to its highest setting, gradually roasting people inside out.

For some people like the old man who had risen with the sun for the past forty-one years to open his newsstand, it was just another hot day. With punctuality only achieved through a meticulous work ethic and "old-school" upbringing from his native land of Guyana, Reggie, as he was known to his customers, arrived on time every day either to see his newspapers and bread being delivered or at least catch a glimpse of the trucks as they sped away. During winter, he would arrive even earlier to shovel snow from the sidewalk and make extra pots of coffee and hot chocolate for his "citizens," as he referred to his loyal batch.

Reggie had known one of these loyalists for over thirty years, having given him his first job at the ripe age of thirteen. The boy purchased a newspaper and bagel on a daily basis, greeting when he arrived and delivering a "Have a nice day" upon leaving. One day, a customer had knocked over the rack of magazines beside the newspapers; the boy placed his paper and bagel on the floor and proceeded to straighten out the mess. Reggie had thanked him and offered a free soda to which the boy replied, "I'd rather work for it." The next day, the boy waited for Reggie by the newsstand, sitting on a stack of newspapers cradling the bread. He would help Reggie setup shop before leaving for school, returning for another four hours until the newsstand closed. Reggie allowed him only four days of work a week, not wanting to interfere with his schooling. "School very important. You get education, you get good job. Make good livin', hones' livin'." He would stare into the lad's eyes. "You do better than me, okay?"

Over the next three years, the two had developed a father-son relationship; Reggie filled the void left behind by the untimely death of the boy's father when he was only six years old. Reggie talked, the boy listened. He even counseled the boy, by then seventeen, on how to ask a girl he had his eye on to the prom, giving the young man a little spending money for the big dance as well. It was as if his own son, of whom he had none, was graduating from high school. And it was soon thereafter that the young man bade farewell to carve out his own niche in life.

The newsstand, which had become a haven for both, became cold and empty. During the first month, Reggie raced to work with hopes of finding the young man waiting with a cup of coffee in hand, only to find a solitary stack of newspapers with several loaves of bread strewn across them like collapsed exclamation points signifying that the lad would not return.

Nine months later, the young man dropped by. Reggie pushed himself from the stool and embraced him like a long lost son, ushering him inside the newsstand, offering a cold drink and half of his sandwich. They talked until closing time, at which point the young man informed his elder that he had just enlisted in the army; Reggie gave him his blessing.

During the four years that the young man was away, he made sure to stop by while on leave and visit his venerable friend, this time over several beers and shots of whiskey. And when he had finished his tour of duty, he used the skills he had learned in the military to land a job in construction. He imagined himself becoming a foreman within five years, but after twenty years on the job, the only real change he saw was in the equipment he used. He had begun with a shovel and then learned how to use the pneumatic jackhammer to break up pavements. From there, he went on to pouring concrete and leveling sidewalks. Soon thereafter, it was gutting buildings, picking up debris and loading it into Dumpsters, putting up Sheetrock, and laying down floors. He got his class B license and heavy equipment operator certificate with hopes of someday working a bucket loader or crane, but the slots were pirated by company men who were in close with the boss. Year after year, he picked up new skills that padded his resume but did nothing by way of promotion or pay scale. Twenty years and half-a-broken body later, he was back to where he had started; except this time he was temporarily breaking up sidewalks like a caveman since generators were constantly overheating during this heat wave; thus air compressors were of little, if any, use.

The young man who spoke of one day owning his own construction company and home was heading down the sidewalk toward the newsstand forty-five minutes later than usual. Reggie peeked over the top of his glasses at the battery-operated clock, confirmed the time with his wristwatch, and watched as the man grabbed a newspaper and approached the counter. Reggie folded his newspaper and smiled.

"Mornin', son." He glanced at the clock. "Sleep late?"

Jacinto sighed and shook his head, placing a dollar bill on the counter.

"You okay?" Reggie's smile faded as he pushed the dollar back, looking at Jacinto who in turn was looking past the magazines into nowhere. "Hey." Reggie patted Jacinto's hand. "Somethin' wrong?"

"Nothing." Jacinto avoided the old man's eyes, staring at the dollar bill in between his hand and Reggie's. "Gotta go." He picked up the newspaper before Reggie could ask another question.

Reggie picked up the money and placed it on the side of the cigar box he used as a cash register. It had been over fifteen years since Jacinto had ever offered to pay for the newspaper; Reggie had stopped charging him. He got off the stool and opened the door to the newsstand, watching his one-time surrogate son disappear into the train station.

Jacinto squeezed the newspaper in the crook of his armpit as he fumbled through his wallet for a credit card, pulling one out while dropping two. He picked them up and swiped the third at the MetroCard dispensing machine to purchase a monthly fair card. The credit card was processed, the machine coughed up a receipt, but no Metrocard. Jacinto looked at the receipt then at the opening where the card should have been dispensed: empty. After several minutes of pressing buttons and swiping another credit card, the machine once again printed the receipt for a purchase but did not spit out a Metrocard. He slapped the dispenser on the side, first mildly then picked up the tempo.

"Yo, my man, you gonna break that shit."

Jacinto looked over his shoulder out of the corner of his eye at the man who had leaned away from the line to look at what he was doing to the machine. A woman sucked her teeth noisily. A thin man with thinning hair and a pinstripe suit a size too big began expressing his discontent with words such as *preposterous*, *ludicrous*, and *absurd*, finally ending with "I would be humiliated not having any money in my account." He straightened his tie and brushed his lapel.

AL BRUNO

Jacinto turned to his electromechanical nemesis, sized it up, and proceeded to deliver a series of front kicks followed by left and right open-hand strikes. People in line cursed and adamantly expressed their contempt at the machine-kicking lunatic. And with every complaint that reached Jacinto's ear, he kicked and punched even harder: the last kick moved the dispenser several inches. The screen flickered then went completely blank. Jacinto closed his eyes and took deep, calculated breaths.

"Shit man!" The man who had leaned out of line to deliver the first comment was now but five feet from Jacinto. "Now look what the fuck you did."

Jacinto opened his eyes, saw two MetroCards in the dispensing slot, picked them up, and walked toward the man.

"I see you got your shit." The man pointed at the cards in Jacinto's hands. "What the fuck are we gonna do?"

"Fuck you." Jacinto locked stares with the man, his nose but an inch from his face. There was more steel in Jacinto's eyes. The man dropped his stare and backed up amid more complaints and cursing.

Jacinto walked past the line of onlookers, staring each of them down; each of them took a step back after he had disarmed their leader, each of them silent. He swiped his MetroCard and proceeded to the far end of the platform, as far away from civilization as possible.

How could he not have seen this coming? There had been several red flags that, looking back, blatantly revealed the growing fondness between his best friend, Valentino, and his wife, Lourdes: the night he awoke to use the bathroom at 3:00 a.m. and found them whispering in the living room three days after he had offered Valentino asylum on his sofa after his wife had kicked him out; the days he had spontaneously called Lourdes to find out that she had not gone to work, which corresponded with Valentino's absences; a sporadic increase in her overtime that even spilled onto a couple of Saturday mornings in order to "catch up on her work"; the decrease in time she spent cooking, claiming to be exhausted from a long day at work, which of course made its way into the bedroom; and finally when he intercepted a credit card bill with purchases made at liquor stores and lingerie, neither of which he had seen. *Who was this mystery man?* He came up empty in every department; even Valentino couldn't provide any answers during their conversations over Reuben sandwiches at lunch and after-work six-packs. Valentino had promised to keep an eye out but warned Jacinto that it was probably nothing, just a phase she was going through. "You know how women are, *mi hermano*," he had advised Jacinto, "*locas como el diablo.*" He was glad he had somebody like Valentino who understood his plight: what a fool he had been.

Jacinto stood on the very edge of the platform, tracing the lights and tracks as they gradually disappeared into the deep, cavernous jaws of the tunnel, conjuring images of an underworld at the end of the line: souls clawing the air helplessly, attempting to pull their burning bodies from lakes of boiling oil; the air itself charged with sulfur and the smell of searing flesh; horned overseers stirring the boiling cauldron of oil, driving back those who made it to the shores with long poles; the bellowing cries of eternal suffering with the raspy, malevolent chortle of scaly, hooved slave masters patrolling the water's edge.

A giant fist of hot air pushed past Jacinto from a train on the opposite side of the tracks, jarring his reverie in pandemonium. If there is a hell, and there was no reason to object otherwise, then he was as close to it now as he ever would be.

Besides the Dantean vision of the devil's domain was there such a thing as a financial hell? If so, then he was up to his knees in boiling oil and gradually descending. How was he going to tell his son who had pinned his acceptance letter to college on his bedroom wall that the money for his college fund had been used to make up the difference on a down payment for their new home? Every last cent of his 401(k) had been lost as well in what was supposed to have been a new beginning in a new home. The dream had been within his grasp yet snatched away like a string of pearls by the tidal wave that had wiped away the life savings of millions of Americans and, with it, dreams that had been achieved and those yet to be.

With a surge of layoffs and employers slashing hours like fat off a pork in order to keep their business afloat, Jacinto lost all the overtime and was placed on a rotating, four-day workweek, turning an already desperate struggle for survival into a downright scramble for existence. Only his seniority and unmatched work ethic—he had been late to work only five times and absent six over the past twenty years—served as the guiding forces that kept his job safe, for now. Eventually, one of the union representatives had commented, work hours would be returned to normal once the recession ended, concluding the meeting by stating that it was imperative for everybody to share the responsibility and come together as one if the company was going to survive.

Initially, Jacinto and others had reluctantly accepted this paltry work schedule: some money is better than no money. But when word leaked that the higher ups had not suffered a pay cut, a near mutiny ensued.

And although they griped and complained like angry toddlers, they were forced to bite their tongues, swallow whatever shred of dignity and pride they had left, and continue working. The men knew that quitting would only benefit management since the acquisition of new workers meant they could start them at a lower pay scale. And with every vacant position, there were thousands of ravenous unemployed people aching to sink their teeth and claws into whatever jobs were available.

But Jacinto was a fighter. Rather than sit back and wallow in self-pity and alcohol, he used the extra time off to work with his uncle at his bodega. Although the pay was one-fifth of what he earned in a day at his job, Uncle Sam would not see a penny of his earnings. Spending time with his uncle, Bernardo Villanueva, turned out to be therapeutic. As Jacinto reminded himself, having the opportunity to work with his uncle could not have come at a better time when both his marriage and dreams had been completely destroyed. As for Bernardo, who had lost his brother, Jacinto's father, when Jacinto was merely six years old, spending time with his nephew brought him closer to his deceased brother. He served as counsel and spiritual advisor to his nephew, warning him not to take action and let things be. "You can't help your son from jail." The words reverberated through Jacinto like a church bell on a Sunday morning, and it took every ounce of energy for him to place aside pride and focus on his son.

For six months, Jacinto worked for Bernardo, enjoying a game of dominos every Friday night with a couple of the regulars who hung out at the bodega. He had finally moved on and was on the verge of mending the relationship with his son, who surprisingly enough did not harbor anger toward his father, when life slapped him with yet another ace of spades: Bernardo lost the bodega.

Jacinto recalled the Friday when he went to the bodega and found his uncle leaning against the counter yelling into the telephone while holding a piece of paper at eye level: it was a letter of foreclosure. The vendors refused to extend him any more credit, demanding payments before any goods were delivered. Soon thereafter, not a single can of beans or gallon of milk entered the store. Less merchandise found its way to the shelves as Bernardo struggled to catch up on payments. But the less merchandise, the less customers. And with fewer customers came less revenue until he was eventually forced to break the bad news to Jacinto, who discovered then and there that his uncle had been in a financial bind for months and was paying him despite the losses. Guilt overcame Jacinto as he figured that had his uncle not taken him in, his wages could have been used for rent and purchasing merchandise. But Bernardo would not allow his nephew to pin the demise of his business on his already troubled soul, claiming that it was all for the better. "I'm old, tired. It's about time for me to enjoy what's left of my life with my family." Jacinto read through the lies. Bernardo even had a final week's pay waiting for Jacinto, who initially declined the envelope, finally caving in as the old man stuffed it into his shirt pocket. "You will offend me if you don't take it." The envelope burned in Jacinto's pocket. Bernardo excused himself to use the bathroom, returning to an empty store and the envelope pinned between the keys of the cash register.

That was over two weeks ago. Jacinto checked on his uncle every day; the old man still had the envelope and told Jacinto that it would remain there until he claimed it. Eventually, he would have to visit Bernardo, who would probably superglue the envelope to his shirt this time around.

The train arrived within ten minutes. Jacinto entered the last car, looked around, spotted an empty seat, sat down, and closed his eyes. An elderly couple boarded the train at the next stop; the wife was being assisted by her husband. Jacinto tapped the husband on the forearm and signaled to his seat. The old man smiled and nodded, but before his wife was able to claim the vacant seat, a young man with headphones slid into it faster than a child grabs a seat in musical chairs. He took out his iPod and began searching for songs.

The circuit breaker inside Jacinto's head tripped once again. Without hesitation, he reached over and grabbed the young man by the neck. Twenty years of muscles that had been trained to shovel, mix cement, and operate jackhammers contracted within his forearms, calloused hands with cement-caked fingernails and knuckles the size of ball-peen hammers came together like a series of hydraulic pistons closing the jaws of a garbage truck, cutting off all oxygen. The iPod swung like a pendulum as the young man pawed helplessly at Jacinto's hand, his face turning a deeper shade of pink then slowly to purple. Tears streamed from his eyes and bubbles of spit escaped the sides of his mouth as a wet spot appeared on his pants.

Jacinto pulled the man to his feet amid mixed chants of approval and alarm, guided him to the door with his iPod dangling from the headphones, and shoved him violently out of the train. The young man fell on all fours clutching at his throat, coughing viciously. The doors closed, and Jacinto turned to the elderly couple; the seat was still unoccupied. He motioned for the old lady to sit down. She looked at her husband, and he nodded. She sat down and smiled at Jacinto.

"God bless you, young man." The husband smiled.

"I hope so." The words echoed through Jacinto's mind. Some passengers smiled and gave him the thumbs-up while others either crossed themselves or shook their heads in disgust. He closed his eyes again and took several more deep breaths.

Work had provided an escape. He welcomed the pickax. Even if the jackhammer was operational, he would have opted for the pickax. There was more satisfaction in "doing it old style" with brute, blue-collar strength than with some air-operated device; it took away some of the old-fashioned work ethic he had grown up around. And to him, his work was all that was left in his pathetic life. Here was dignity. Here was, as Reggie constantly reminded him, an honest day's work. And every man must earn his keep by the sweat of his brow.

He sat on a palette of plywood away from the rest of the workers, and when the foreman dropped by to ask where the fuck his buddy Valentino was, Jacinto told him to fuck off, threw away the remainder of his coffee, got up, and left, leaving the foreman with his hands on his hips and a look of bewilderment on his face. The last person the foreman had ever expected to curse at him was Jacinto. He scratched his head and went back to the trailer. There was no point in writing him up; Jacinto was just having a bad day.

Neil

Neil first applied a mineral-rich cleanser made out of green tea, Irish moss, and kelp on his face that eliminated free radicals while providing essential nutrients, which repaired damaged skin. This was followed by a soothing aftershave, which also served as a cleansing toner, made from rose hip and chamomile, reducing inflammation, redness, and blemishes caused by shaving. Next, a lotion infused with a mixture of vitamins A and B, and coenzyme Q10, which not only delayed premature aging, but aided in the treatment of rosacea. Finally, to shield himself from stress factors and air pollutants, he gently applied a moisturizer with a jojoba base in small circles that acted as an astringent; this also helped reduce bumps and irritation, leaving the skin taut and smooth. He rinsed his hands, reached for hair gel, scooped a fair amount, divided it onto both hands, and massaged it into his hair with his fingertips before combing it back evenly. He leaned forward and looked for any visible nose hairs, finishing with several splashes of Cartier Roadster aftershave lotion complimented by Cartier Declaration cologne.

He fussed over two pairs of cuff links: platinum and the onyx with diamonds in the middle. He put one on each sleeve then looked in the mirror; the onyx would match the onyx tie clip with his initials stamped in white gold. Today's theme was "dashing": $425 Michael Kors linen suit, $75 Calvin Klein shirt, $80 Alfani tie, $148 Cole Haan Plain Toe Oxfords, and for the pièce de résistance a $475 Burberry stainless steel wristwatch.

The middle-aged Wall Street realtor scrutinized his appearance from head to toe in front of his wife's full-length mirror, making several half turns, readjusting his tie three times before donning his blazer. He grabbed his $295 Kenneth Cole New York Durango Flap Portfolio Briefcase, car keys, and descended the stairs of his six-bedroom, three-and-a-half bathroom, two-story house in Poughkeepsie.

"Honey, I'm leaving," he yelled as he walked to the front door.

"Remember to pick up some wine for tonight. Stacy and Keith are coming over tonight," his wife yelled from the kitchen.

"That's tonight?" He stopped at the door. "It's Thursday."

"I know, I know." His wife stuck her head out from the kitchen. "They can't make it tomorrow. 'Sides, Ryan's got soccer practice tomorrow. Love you." She blew a kiss and disappeared.

"Okay," he sighed. Canceling tonight's plans would allow him a couple of extra hours at work to finish up a huge property deal he had been working on for quite some time, but having company over the weekend would be even worse. "Sure."

Neil drove his Mercedes-Benz to the Metro-North station and used the Park-n-Ride to commute into Manhattan. He had driven his car into Lower Manhattan once, but after being greeted by a plethora of traffic jams, red lights, potholes, jaywalking-happy pedestrians, incessant horn-honking, and near fender benders with crazed cabbies cutting each other off to pick up passengers, he vowed never to drive into "mayhem central" ever again. Besides, the air-conditioned cabs on the train provided a comforting, stress-free commute. Not to mention the possibility of his car overheating during this heat wave.

Sweat and Neil were the worst of enemies. At least six T-shirts and six spare dress shirts were kept on reserve in his office along with duplicate bottles of cologne from home and at least three bars of deodorant along with toothpaste, toothbrush, and a grooming kit. He would change T-shirts at midday every day. And on hot summer days, he would walk about like Mary Poppins with an oversized parasol. "Sweat and bad odor," he would tell his secretary, "are for barbarians."

Despite the blazing temperatures, today promised to be a good day. His company had acquired some valuable real estate in the Upper East

Side of Manhattan, where it planned to finance the construction of two condominiums. Neil had personally handled the acquisition of the property by buying out a couple of bodegas, a Chinese restaurant, a dilapidated hardware store, a third-rate insurance company, two liquor stores, and three nail salons. At first the store owners were vehemently opposed to moving, claiming that they had built their businesses through hard work and sweat and that they planned on keeping with the tradition by passing it on to their kids. Neil presented them with a lucrative package, but some declined. So he smiled and went to work behind closed doors, calling friends in high places that could exert pressure on the business owners. By then the recession that began in 2008 was in full bloom, and once Neil saw that they were hurting, he moved in like a rabid, yet silent wolf, again offering to purchase their properties; this time the amount on the checks was less. Again the storeowners refused, preferring to tighten their seatbelts, wait out the turbulent storm, and ask for mercy from the financial gods. But as the economy withered, so too did their finances. Merchandise could not be bought, and rents could not be paid. In the end, they were forced to hand over their properties to Neil, who watched while sipping cappuccinos as they signed on the dotted line. This time around, the numbers on the checks were even lower than the second visit, and of course, Uncle Sam would get his fair share. The last person to sign over his property, a Senor Villanueva, who had owned a bodega for over thirty-nine years, spat at Neil's feet, calling him a "*demonio blanco*."

"Don't worry, Mister, where you go after you die, everything is always hot. Vallase al infierno, so hijo de puta."

"Thank you, Mr. Villanueva. I'll take that into consideration. Have a nice day." He waved goodbye and swatted the air. "And buy some soap with that check please."

Neil grabbed the cellular phone from his belt, flipped it open, and pressed a couple of numbers.

"Holly, yes, it's me. Patch me through to Evans." He locked the door and walked around the empty store, staying clear from the dirt-covered shelves, stepping over a torn bag of rice and crushed boxes of pasta. A calendar with a picture of a cockfight hung behind the antiquated, push-button register. Several other pictures of saints adorned the wall next to an empty potato-chip rack; a 5 x 7 inch picture of the Virgin Mary stared back at Neil.

"Evans, yeah, it's done. Put the T-bones on the grill, get the caviar ready, and break open the champagne." He ended the phone call, wiped his hands, and straightened his tie before taking one last look at the picture of the Virgin Mary.

"Hey, it's only business." He made a pistol gesture at the photograph and winked. "Nothing personal."

An hour later, Neil floated into his air-conditioned office with a grin from ear to ear as if he had just uncovered the true identity of the shooter at the grassy knoll. He winked at his secretary who informed him that he had several messages from the same customers that had been trying to get a hold of him for the past two weeks. Neil had cashed in on property loans he had approved to dream-happy customers whose credit was no better than their English. When the market collapsed, they sought Neil for support and explanations. But he cunningly evaded their phone calls, giving them the usual run-around while having his secretary wear out the phrases "He just stepped out of the office about five minutes ago. You just missed him." When one of his customers showed up unexpectedly at his office, he smiled and listened with the interest of a two-year-old at a tax audit, took copious nonsense notes, and promised to "work diligently to solve the problem." As time dragged on, the task of informing them that there was absolutely nothing he could do to solve their problems fell in the hands of his secretary for fifteen years, who constantly warned him of the consequences of goading people into loans guaranteed to fail.

*   *   *

The Hottest Day

There exists no painting, no photograph, no poem that has been able to capture the beauty of a sunrise: bulging hues of white and yellow bands pushing upward a cornucopia of blues embellished with cottony strokes, themselves pushing against a sea of fiery reds and oranges peeking from behind clouds, which in turn collided with deeper tones of purples. With every new day comes a rebirth of the soul, a cleansing process promising a new beginning, a reaffirmation of life, confirming one's existence—*I am here, I have arrived!*

But Jacinto saw none of this as he dragged his cement-laden feet across the sidewalk, tracing the ground with his eyes, staring at the constellation of gums, wondering about the people that had placed them there. Every gum told a tale. Every blotch had once been part of a life. *Who were these people? What had they been thinking while chewing their gum?* Once the flavor had been sapped, once it was no longer of any use, it had been expelled from their mouths and onto the floor. He was one of them. His life, his thoughts, were somewhere on the sidewalk, sharing space among other past lives. His life had lost its flavor; there was very little meaning to his existence.

Wall Street seemed to be affected the most by the heat wave as air wrestled to find its way around the colossal labyrinth of cement and steel, where Titans loomed menacingly over their undersized counterparts. These behemoths forced their way upward, defying each other's existence, staring at one another from across streets at a distance of a mere hundred feet or so between them; obelisks of rock and iron with hundreds of glass eyes converging at the lower tip of Manhattan, forging a citadel replica comparable to Mount Olympus. Yet the gods that dwelled within these monolithic towers ruled with pens rather than lightning bolts.

It was on a Friday when the mercury reached 106 degrees, matching the hottest day recorded in history, July 9, 1936. People were advised not to stay in the sun for too long, wear sunblock if working outside, and drink plenty of water; the latter fueling street entrepreneurs into selling bottles of water at almost every street corner of the Big Apple. Children, old folks, and pets were to be monitored constantly and given at least a gallon of water throughout the day. Thousands hit the streets in an attempt to escape the furnacelike ambient of their homes, only to find themselves stepping out into a larger furnace. And in an area such as Wall Street where buildings barricaded what little breeze came from either river, the air was suffocating. A person would expel a breath of hot air only to replace it with a fresh breath of even hotter air.

Jacinto was at work at Chambers Street, hacking away at the asphalt with a pickax; the generator had overheated preventing the use of air-operated jackhammers. Chunks flew as the pointed end of the ax struck the ground. He envisioned Valentino's face on the asphalt with every blow.

Sparks flew as the pickax struck the cement, sending debris flying violently in various directions as Jacinto's frenzy escalated. A chunk the size of a quarter struck Neil's briefcase. He stopped, closed his umbrella, ran a hand across the briefcase, and shot a menacing look at the sweat-soaked brute with the pickax.

"Hey buddy! Watch what you're doing, okay?" Neil massaged the area on the briefcase. "Asshole."

Jacinto rested the pickax on his shoulder and stared at the suit, chest heaving, the grip on the handle tightening, highlighting the veins on his hand and the tribulations of veins and muscles in his arms.

"What's the matter? Deaf or something? Moron." Neil turned to walk away.

Twenty years. Twenty stinking years and nothing to show for it, not even a wife. Jacinto made his way around the broken sidewalk, pushed aside the barrier, and walked toward the man.

"You touch me and I'll sue you." Neil looked at Jacinto from head to toe. "And from the looks of it, you'd better think twice. I seriously doubt you can afford it." He grinned in victory.

Jacinto weighed his options as much as he weighed the pickax, swinging it gently like a pendulum at his side. He looked up at the man.

"You're right, Val. I don't have any money left. Besides, you even took my Lourdes." He raised the pickax over his shoulder with both hands and swung it forward.

Neil dropped the briefcase and made a futile attempt at shielding himself from the jagged spike that found its way through his arms and into his eye. The point of the pickax erupted through the back of his head. His twitching body fell backward with the pickax extending from his head like a tree branch. The legs danced for several seconds before making one final stretch. Jacinto placed his foot on the man's forehead and wiggled the ax free as it made a sucking noise. A mixture of gray matter, blood, and tissue oozed from the eye socket.

Jacinto stood above the corpse and placed a foot on his chest. He leaned over and pulled out the handkerchief from the man's blazer and wiped his brow.

"Damn it's hot, eh, Val?"

A hot gust of wind slammed into Reggie's face as he emerged from the subway station, hotter than usual, signifying the beginning of what promised to be, as is said, "a scorcher." Record-setting temperatures had plagued the city for over a week and a half, but something about today's heat, within the heat, that carried with it a portentous feeling as if walking through a graveyard at night. Could today finally be the day in which the sun inches closer to us? Just enough to purge mankind of its sins, incinerating the spiritual along with the physical with just a mere increase in several more degrees?

Reggie tugged at his collar and loosened yet another button. He brought, as he had over the past week, spare T-shirts, shirts, along with handkerchiefs. If mankind's judgment arrived today, he'd make sure he'd greet St. Peter with fresh clothes.

AL BRUNO

He walked over to the stack of newspapers—the bread had not been delivered—leaned to pick it up, and gasped. Trembling fingers fumbled with the string, finally yanking one of the papers free.

CRAZED MAN MURDERS WALL STREET BUSINESSMAN

The paper shook in his hands as an 8 x 10 inch colored photograph of Jacinto stared back at him from the splash page. He read briefly before collapsing on the stack of newspapers. Tears mixed in with the sweat that already adorned his face. The paper fell silently at his feet and remained there as there was no breeze to carry the bad news away. The old man covered his face and wept for several minutes before retracing his steps to the subway station. For the first time in over forty years, Reggie's newsstand did not open.

THE TREEHOUSE

THE NEWS

We did not dare to breathe a prayer
Or give our anguish scope!
Something was dead in each of us,
And what was dead was Hope!
　　　—Oscar Wilde, *The Ballad of Reading Gaol*

January 19, 1996, 6:03 p.m.

"UP AHEAD ON tonight's top stories, the fertility wonder drug Fertilisure, initially heralded as the answer to infertility, has been officially banned by the FDA as reports of stillborn births and deformed babies rise across the country. The FDA has ordered an immediate halt to the production and distribution of the drug, claiming that it has been directly linked to dozens of these cases. Dr. Nathan Wellington, head of internal medicine and leading research scientist from the FDA, had this to say about the drug:"

"Infertility is a common thing in about 10-20 percent of couples in America. Although it is not a life-threatening ailment, the psychological effects on women are almost equal. Denying a woman the heavenly gift of motherhood can be quite traumatic and downright painful: infertility does just that. Unable to bear children, many women feel incomplete, thus falling into profound states of depression, suicide, and in some cases, psychosis.

"However, there are certain treatments and processes that can be carried out which enable a woman to have babies. In vitro fertilization, a procedure in which egg cells are fertilized by sperm outside of the womb, is perhaps the most popular; adoption second. But for some parents who want the child to be 'theirs,' these two methods are not an option. This is where drugs such as Fertilisure come in selling improbable dreams to eager victims. Although drugs such as these produce promising results in laboratories, they are a far cry from the solution. And Fertilisure epitomizes dreams of grandeur from both its creators and women. The end results are, as you can see, quite tragic. This is in turn can plunge—and most often does—women into an even greater state of disillusionment. In the end, Fertilisure promised dreams but delivered nightmares."

"Doctors are urging women to stay away from Fertilisure until the FDA has completed its investigations. Women currently taking the drug are being urged by doctors to stop immediately and call the number at the bottom of the screen for more information. All calls will be kept confidential. Until then, officials say, artificial insemination and adoption are the safest and most viable options."

ATHENA

Yet we met; and fate bound us
together at the altar; and I never spoke of passion, nor thought
of love. She, however, shunned society, and, attaching herself
to me alone, rendered me happy. It is a happiness to wonder;—
It is a happiness to dream.

—Edgar Alan Poe, *Morella*

CRAIG RAISED ATHENA by himself. By the time she turned two, she began to reject the milk and regular baby food. She was beginning to get awfully thin, and this concerned him. The bones on her legs and arms, especially her collarbones, pushed against her skin. He didn't know what else to feed her. One night while burping her, she licked his shoulder and sank her teeth into his flesh. He yelled and pulled her off: she was licking blood from her lips. An hour later, he was back at the tree house with a bag of raw chicken. Athena tore open the bag like a piñata with her little claws and stripped the flesh from the bones in seconds. Craig sat back and watched amid a mixture of apprehension and fascination. Ever since then, her diet consisted of raw chicken and meat. And when she got older, he began to find the skeletal remains of cats, rodents, birds, and stray dogs tossed in a pile in a corner of the tree house. These he would gather in a bag and bury them about two hundred yards out.

As the years passed, a strong father-daughter relationship developed. She loved to play tag and gnaw on a basketball he had bought her; it had been deflated the very first night when she sunk her teeth into it. These games took place at night. Keen olfactory senses allowed her to anticipate her father's arrival. He would break into the clearing, and there she was, crouched at the base of the tree, her eyes a pair of moonlit orbs that interrupted the darkness of the woods. She would grunt and pounce on him. He looked forward to these warm greetings. However, as she doubled in size and tripled in strength, he constantly found himself careening backward and hitting the ground with such force that it would knock the wind out of him. This would immediately be followed by a cascade of licks from a thick course tongue that left his face soaked in saliva. Then there were the ripped shirts and scratch marks left by her claws, which initially sparked several arguments with his wife. A thick welder's jacket and an occasional manicure had prevented further scratches. They would play first then eat. Athena loved soda. They would share one with every meal, and Craig would cry with laughter as she made faces and burped from the carbonated drink.

Athena was his only child, a wretch born under a shroud of calamity. To the world she would be labeled an abomination. But to Craig who had become accustomed to her extreme deformities, she was his flesh, his child, his daughter. He bestowed her with all the love and care that a parent can give, his blood coursed through her veins. She was his life, his penance.

He would visit her as often as possible, sometimes every night. And only he knew of her existence, taking every precautionary measure possible to maintain her hidden from the outside world.

AL BRUNO

BIRTH

May the strong curse of crossed affections light
Back on thy bosom with reflected blight!
And make thee in thy leprosy of mind
As loathsome to thyself as to mankind!
—Percy Bysshe Shelley, *To the Lord Chancellor*

July 14, 1995, 8:47 p.m.
"HONEY, COULD YOU bring me some more ginger ale?"
Susannah winced as she struggled to find a comfortable position on the couch. She took a deep breath and grabbed a handful of popcorn. A kernel fell on her shirt. She picked it up and placed it on her tongue.

"Here you go." Craig leaned over the back of the couch and handed her the glass. A small whimper escaped her as she shifted her weight once again. He frowned. "Are you okay?"

"I . . . I don't know." Susannah shifted again, took another deep breath, and placed her hand on her belly. She set the cup on the table and probed her swollen belly with both hands like a gypsy reading a crystal ball.

"Honey, are you okay?" He made his way around the furniture and kneeled in front of her, watching as she caressed her belly.

The phone rang. Craig let it ring.

Susannah pursed her lips. "Whoever it is, I'm sleeping."

He hesitated; the phone kept ringing.

"Please, pick it up." She grabbed her belly and shut her eyes.

He reached over and grabbed the receiver while massaging her knee with his left hand, eyes riveted to hers.

"Hello . . . Larry? How are you?" Susannah began to breathe heavier. "Yeah, uh, listen, Larry, let me call you back." She groaned. "I don't know. Tomorrow." He hung up and grabbed both of her hands; they were clammy. "Oh boy, uh . . ." He licked his lips. "Uh, yeah."

"Oh, Craig." She writhed and placed both of her hands at her sides as if trying to push herself up from the sofa. "Craig." Her breathing intensified with every breath. "CRAIG!" She pulled back on her blouse and placed her hands on her belly; a small bump appeared and was gone just as quickly. Craig stared at the Himalayan flesh that had once been his wife's belly.

She grabbed his hands and placed them in the area where the push had originated. His hands were trembling; she stroked them. "It's okay."

He took a deep breath.

"Feel it?" She smiled.

Craig cocked his head and leaned closer. The push came again. His hands recoiled, and his lips quivered. He placed his hands on her belly again waiting for another kick. The pounding became more frequent: the life inside wanted out.

"Oh baby." Susannah's face reddened as she shut her eyes. "I think it's time."

Craig hopped to his feet and began darting in and out of rooms. Every little detail had been carefully planned out for over four months. As the days kept falling off the calendar, he had increased his weekly inspection of the emergency bag—which started out as a traveling bag and metamorphosed into a duffel bag—to a daily basis: pajamas, check; toothbrush, check; toothpaste, check; soap with plastic case, check; slippers, check; hairbrush, check; towel, check; panties and bras, check; and two disposable cameras, double check. Susannah had given up telling him that everything was going to be okay, that she was not going off on some expedition in search of Livingstone. "I know, I know," he would respond, only to recheck the bag the following day. After a while, it had become rather amusing. "Honey, don't forget to check the bag." This would send him scrambling to conduct yet another inventory.

The time had now arrived. Craig rechecked the bag and decided that there were a couple of items missing. He ran to the kitchen, grabbed two plastic cups, shoved them into the bag, sprinted to the bathroom, and emerged cradling half a dozen bottles of pills from pain relievers to cough suppressants.

"Honey, it's a hospital." Susannah sighed and shook her head as he continued the scavenger hunt, opening and closing cabinets and slamming drawers. He came out juggling bottles of perfumes in his left hand, a cellular phone in the right hand, pressed to his ear, a can of hairspray bulging out of his front left pocket, and her curling iron in his right rear pocket with the extension cord dragging behind like a whip.

"Barnaby, meet us at the hospital. Susannah's having the baby." Pause. "Yes, right now." He shoved the phone into his shirt pocket.

"Babe." The pounding in her womb cut short her laughter as she smiled nervously. "I think you got everything." She closed her eyes. "Can we please go!"

Craig punched the items into the bag and fought with the zipper. The extension cord hung from the half-opened bag like a tail. He threw it on his shoulder, snatched the keys from the counter, and ran out the door. The pictures by the entrance shook.

"Craig?" Susannah heard the car start and waited. Tires screeched as he revved the engine. She looked over her shoulder. The sound of the car's engine faded down the street. About a minute later, she heard tires screeching onto the driveway and a loud metallic clang as the garbage cans toppled over. A car door slammed. Keys jingled outside the door. Craig slammed open the door, knocking a picture to the floor, sending shards of glass in all directions.

"Shit!" He ran to Susannah.

She looked up at him and smiled. "Did you forget something?"

"Sorry," he smiled an apology.

9:31 p.m.

The night air was crisp, serene, and almost pure. Its soothing coolness seemed to penetrate the skin without interfering with the warmth inside. The streetlights shone in silence and radiated even brighter; they too enjoyed the genteel comfort of the night. Earth's satellite hovered just within the reach of the imagination, itself a luminescent shield of splendor accentuating the sublime evening as sedated waves danced in the Sea of Tranquility.

Wails of sirens from two police cars that appeared to be chasing one another jarred Barnaby's reverie. He secured the zipper on his navy-blue windbreaker. The phone call had interrupted what otherwise would have been a long and very much deserved night's sleep. He had left his house with the same clothes he had worn all day: jeans and a pair of boat shoes. For over thirty years, he had been receiving emergency phone calls at all hours of the day and treated every one as if it was his first, yet this one was special. He puffed on his pipe and checked his watch while pacing outside the emergency room entrance. An ambulance pulled up, made a U-turn, and began to back up with a loud chirping. Barnaby walked over as the driver got out, ran to the back of the ambulance, and slid out the collapsible gurney. He stepped closer and took a drag from his pipe. The wheels on the gurney locked and an elderly black man with cotton hair and a respirator mask attached to a small green canister of oxygen at his side was wheeled into the emergency room. One of the paramedics assisted an elderly woman out of the back. A burgundy nightgown sprouted from the bottom of her tan wool coat. She had on slippers. Her teary eyes met Barnaby's for a second before she vanished into the hospital. He sighed and walked away while checking his watch.

Craig scanned the people as he pulled into the emergency room traffic circle. He saw the man in the blue windbreaker and beeped his horn. The old man waved and made his way to the curb. Craig pulled up and rolled down the window on the passenger's side. "Barnaby, thanks for coming." He got out of the car.

"Susannah dear, how are you?" Barnaby opened the passenger's side door and held out his hand. "Are you ready?"

She took a deep breath and forced a smile.

"Good. Wait here. I'll get a wheelchair." He disappeared through the sliding doors and, seconds later, emerged with a wheelchair, locked the wheels, and sat her down.

"I'll be right in." Craig kissed her on the forehead. "Gotta find some parking. Don't start without me."

"It's not up to me anymore." She patted her belly.

After ten minutes of zigzagging and braking through the parking lot like a pinball, Craig finally found parking and raced back frantically, his heart a wrecking ball pounding away at his chest. He ran into the emergency room as if having crossed the finish line of the Boston Marathon, approached the receptionist at the nurses' station, and slammed a fist on the counter.

"I'm going into labor!"

The security guard dropped his newspaper and catapulted from his seat as Craig pounded away like a doomsday prophet. He walked over to Craig, placed a hand on his shoulders, and suggested he take it easy and that everything was going to be okay.

Minutes later, the security guard escorted him to the delivery room on the second floor. In the five minutes or so that it took to get to the delivery room, Craig had been schooled on the joys of fatherhood especially the experience of the firstborn. He learned about seventeen-year-old Monica, who aspired to be a fashion designer; fifteen-year-old Leonard, who loved to collect basketball cards as well as porno magazines; and the thirteen-year-old twins, Kimberly and Ashley; Kimberly needed braces and Ashley had been caught smoking weed in the bathroom.

"It's good to have a family," the security guard remarked as he smiled and wished Craig all the luck in the world. "Society needs good fathers." He gave Craig a thumbs-up and walked away.

9:52 p.m.

"Here, put these on, Mr. Russo." One of the nurses handed Craig a pair of scrubs in a sealed plastic bag. He clawed at the bag and put them on in haste, complaining about the fit. The nurse informed him that the gown was on backwards. He took it off, looked at it, and slipped it back on; the nurse fastened it at the back. She smiled and handed him a paper cap and a mask. "Follow me."

He followed her into the delivery room. There were two more nurses: one of them was inspecting the oxygen tanks and checking the tubing while the other arranged towels and surgical equipment on a cart. He caught a glimpse of Susannah buried under light-blue sheets with her legs in stirrups, blowing enough air to put out the Olympic torch. She saw him approach and attempted a smile that depicted pain rather than happiness.

"Hi, honey," she began to sob.

"Come, come." Barnaby turned around and waved him over.

Craig approached the bed. He leaned over and kissed Susannah, wiping away some of the sweat on her forehead, tucking her hair back into the cap. She had always had a strong grip, but the adrenaline in her was quadrupled, and when she grabbed his hand, he did his best not to yell.

"I love you," he whispered into her ear.

She smiled, and this time happiness shone through but quickly metamorphosed into a mask of pain as a powerful contraction hit her. Her body stiffened, and the veins in her neck bulged, face turning a deeper shade of red. Craig winced and worked his hand free: the skin on the back of his hand had been peeled off, revealing four red crescent shapes where the fingernails had dug in. He looked about helplessly. The nurses sprang into action. The oxygen mask was placed on her nose and mouth, and she was instructed to take deep breaths and relax. Susannah complied until another contraction hit her. Barnaby positioned himself. For a moment there, Craig thought he was going to yell "Hike!" He was a bit apprehensive of having someone—in this case a close friend—spread his wife's legs apart like a wishbone and insert their fingers into her swollen vagina as if probing for a missing ring. The anesthesiologist checked the levels on the gauges and glanced at the heart monitor as she gently stroked Susannah's head. "You're doing fine." A smile cracked underneath her mask. Susannah let out more tears, which the nurse tenderly brushed away.

"Okay, Susan, listen to me. You're doing a great job." Barnaby's tender voice even managed to soothe Craig. Susannah fixed her eyes on him and nodded. "Are you ready?" She nodded quickly. "Good. Now, we're going to help you, but you're the director and have to do most of the work. When I tell you to push, you push. When I tell you to hold, you hold. And when I tell you to relax and take a deep breath, you do it. Do you think you could do that for us?" She blinked and nodded. "Excellent. Okay, ready?" He paused. "Push."

Craig inadvertently closed his eyes, held his breath, and began to push, matching grips with his wife. Rivulets of sweat raced down his forehead, face as crimson as hers.

"Okay, relax. Breathe."

Craig expelled a gush of air and felt the bones in his legs bend like plastic straws. He quickly steadied himself and cleared his throat. Two of the nurses looked at each other in amusement. He blinked several times and shook his head.

"Good job, both of you," Barnaby uttered. One of the nurses snickered. Over the next ten minutes, Susannah pushed, held, relaxed, took deep breaths, and repeated the ritual. Craig's breathing relaxed, but his heart was still pounding away like a jackhammer on a city sidewalk. She was administered oxygen several times and managed to crack a smile every so often. Barnaby continued to reassure her that she was doing fine, remaining stoic and as calm as when he had started.

"Push, push," Craig echoed Barnaby.

"Once again. Take a deep breath, hold it, and push," Barnaby demanded.

She scowled, held her breath, and pushed, defecating in the process. One of the nurses handed Barnaby a damp wipe. He cleaned the area without so much as flinching and resumed his commands. "Push, sweetheart. You're doing fine, Susannah, just fine. Almost there."

Susannah gave one last push and nearly fainted. Her sanguine features replaced by a pale, waxen shade of pink. The nurse readjusted the oxygen mask as her eyes rolled back. Craig looked at Barnaby and made his way around the bed to see his child with lead in his legs, becoming entangled in the wiring. One of the nurses unraveled him. By the time he was free, Barnaby was frowning. The nurse closest to him sucked in her mask as she gasped and brought a hand to her chest.

"What's wrong?" Craig stiffened. "Barnaby?"

"*Quickly, quickly!*" Barnaby snapped his fingers. One of the nurses slipped him a scalpel while another ran to the phone.

The room began to spin for Craig. His jaw twitched as the floor began to shrink. He reached out for support and grabbed a handful of plastic

AL BRUNO

tubing that stretched into Susannah's arms, snapping them and sending an I.V. bag to the floor with the tail whipping around like a viper.

A nurse screamed as she wiped blood from her face.

Craig felt something drip on his forehead. He wiped away the area and came away with blood. The nurse who screamed was standing at his side patching the gash in Susannah's arm that had been caused by the needle that had been ripped out.

"Are you okay?" She grabbed Craig by the arm and helped him to his feet.

He braced himself on the handrails and ran a trembling hand across his mouth. There was very little movement from his wife. She was quite pale, the mask fogged with every breath she took. Barnaby had his back turned to him; the other two nurses were opposite of him on a small table. All three were looking down at something.

A heart-shaped icon flashed on and off on an overhead monitor; besides the flashing heart were big green numbers counting down: 98 . . . 97 . . . 96 . . . . A yellow line spiked every couple of seconds on a horizontal screen just below. Craig traced one of the lines from the monitor to Susannah's right index finger. He placed a quivering hand on hers and squeezed. A tear fell on her hand.

He jumped as three doctors—one male and two females—barged in. Barnaby motioned them over like a traffic cop as the nurses stepped aside. The male doctor waved one of the nurses over, said something that Craig did not catch, and sent her scrambling to the medicine cabinet. She hurried back and handed over a bottle and a syringe. Craig hobbled over to get a closer look.

The doctor tapped the syringe and depressed the plunger, gazing at the thin miniature geyser as it shot into the air. Craig followed the needle with his eyes as it disappeared into a tiny arm. Barnaby began pushing up and down gently on the chest of the fragile body. He did this several times before leaning over and pressing his mouth to the child's bluish-purple lips. His cheeks puffed up as if he were blowing a conch shell.

"Barnaby . . ." Craig's voice trailed off in a whisper. The floor began to disappear once again. *Not again. Stay strong! Stay in control!* He fought the gelatinous feeling in his legs. *Get a grip, get a grip.* A small wail escaped him as he straightened up. Barnaby and two of the nurses turned to him. He caught Barnaby's stare: horror stared back. Barnaby turned back to the body. Craig watched helplessly as the doctors attempted to breathe life into the body of his child. The nurses darted to and from the medicine cabinet, crash cart, and sink. The mayhem continued for what seemed an eternity before one of the female doctors placed a stethoscope to the chest and an ear to the mouth of the tiny body. She pressed her fingers on the neck, looking at Barnaby who appeared as if he had just walked in from the rain. She pursed her lips, sighed, and shook her head. Two of the nurses hugged while the third crossed herself. The male doctor ran a hand across his forehead and took a deep breath as the other female doctor crossed her arms and merely stared at the lifeless child.

Craig became a piece of stalagmite. Barnaby turned slowly to face him, shoulders sagged. The hair on his arms was pasted against his skin. His entire shirt was wet. All conversation ceased. The intercom went silent. No more machines were being wheeled about. Nothing. Craig continued to listen for the wailing of his child, but it never came.

"Craig . . . I . . . I'm sorry." Barnaby dragged his feet, pausing to stare into Craig's eyes. "There was nothing we could do, nothing we could do." He laced his hands in prayer. "I'm so sorry."

Craig regarded his wife. *Oh, Suzy . . .*

Minutes later, the staff began to clear. One of the nurses pushed the crash cart gently toward the wall while another checked Susannah's vitals. The third nurse cupped her mouth with a trembling hand, eyes puffy from tears cascading down her cheeks. Craig took a deep breath and unglued his legs from the floor. Every step he took felt as if he was dragging a sack of cement across asphalt. Barnaby stepped to the side. There before him lay the inanimate body of his child. It was a girl. Her mouth was contoured into a small O in a futile attempt for air that had been denied; the arms were slightly folded across her chest. He searched for a response, for feelings, for something, but found nothing. Pain and anger settled in.

Who is this child? Is this my little girl? Who was she going to be later on in life? This is my daughter. This can't be my daughter! Susannah. Our child is dead. Our child is dead.

"Craig." Barnaby placed a hand on Craig's shoulder with slight conviction. "There was nothing we could do."

Craig cleared his throat and wiped his eyes. "W-what happened?"

"The umbilical cord was wrapped around her neck." He paused to look at the body. "There was nothing we could have done. Please understand."

Craig zombied over to Susannah. Her eyes were half-open, her skin pale, damp, and deathly cold. She looked at Craig, blinked several times, and closed her eyes.

"Hey." She smiled weakly.

"Hey," Craig responded. His lower jaw trembled. He looked over his shoulder. "I'd like to be alone with my wife for a minute."

Barnaby ushered the nurses out. Craig summoned him as he was about to exit the room. He sauntered over to Craig and stood beside him waiting to be sentenced, unable to muster enough energy or courage to look at Craig. Silence served as the verdict, neither man could meet the other's eyes: one could find neither strength nor words; the other carried a cross on his back.

Craig cleared his throat. "Listen, I . . ."

Susannah began to groan and writhe in pain. The numbers on the monitor increased along with the frequency of spikes on the yellow line. She grabbed the handrails and pushed. Her eyelids fluttered as if she were experiencing a nightmare of biblical proportions. As Craig reached for her hand, Susannah's eyes shot open, and she sat up violently. He jumped and nearly took the surgical equipment cart with him; several instruments and a small banana-shaped stainless steel container clanged on the tiles. She clutched his shirt and pulled him toward her ripping chest hairs. Craig winced and grabbed a hold of her wrist. Barnaby rushed to the other side and helped restrain Susannah. Her eyes overfilled with anguish and fear as she gulped oxygen. The blips on the monitor sounded like a distress signal in Morse code.

"Susannah, please! You must calm down," Barnaby pleaded as he pressed against her shoulders. Her body had gone rigid as if thousands of volts were racing through her body.

"Dammit!" Craig reached over and grabbed a handful of Barnaby's shirt. "Do something!"

While Barnaby fought against the couple, Susannah's body slackened until she was back to groaning. He pushed Craig's hand away. "Please, you too!" He took a deep breath. "I need you to remain calm."

"Dammit!" Craig ran a quivering hand over his face. He pumped a fist in the air like a gavel and pressed a thumb into his temple. "Shit."

Susannah stirred violently and began to push with all her might. Her face reddened and the veins on her neck and temples ballooned like tributaries on the Nile. She placed both hands on her belly and raised her head. "Oh, God . . . ," she managed to squeeze out in between breaths.

Craig leaned forward, staring at Susannah's vagina as it gradually widened to expose the top of what appeared to be a head. "Barnaby . . ." his voice but a hoarse whisper.

"Dear God!" Barnaby circled the table, darted to the crash cart, grabbed a pair of gloves and a scalpel, and returned even quicker. "Move!" He pushed

Craig with his shoulder. "Okay, Suzy, we've got one more round. Let's go, sweetheart. You and me. Just like before."

Susannah did not respond. She nodded weakly with her eyes closed. Droplets of sweat adorned her pallid face like early morning dew on the petal of a white rose. Her arms went limp as her body relaxed with a final sigh of exhaustion.

"Susannah?" Barnaby sighed and gently placed his hands on the head of the infant.

Craig swallowed hard; his soul had been recharged. The final chapter would not be written as an epitaph; the story would continue.

Barnaby pulled gently on the slimy head. Craig's heart raced as a nervous smile formed on his face. Shoulders and arms appeared. His smile began to fade. Barnaby frowned and mumbled. Icy tendrils crept through Craig's skin like a virus gone mad. When the doctor had finally pulled the legs free and turned *it* over, dread pierced Craig's heart, rooted itself there, and spread a deathly chill throughout his body. Barnaby bobbled the abomination in his hands as if he were handling sin, finally setting *it* down between Susannah's legs with the umbilical cord snaking into her womb. He took a step back and collided with the crash cart toppling it over: scissors, scalpels, clamps, and other surgical equipment clattered to the floor. He stared at the blood as it dripped from his fingertips, staggered over to the sink and peeled off the plastic gloves violently, spackling the mirror and white tiles with droplets of blood. He leaned over and buried his face under the water.

Craig heard him vomit violently as he stared at the bloodstained spawn. Its fingers curved into fleshy claws crowned by fingernails shaped like hooks. Deformed legs modeled after a satyr. Bony ridges ran up and down its spine, culminating in a pronounced hump at the base of the neck that was slightly covered with hair. The misshapen head was adorned with scattered tufts of hair. Then there was the face: reptilian orbs resembling pools of amber pus and nose like a bat's. It was another female.

Craig approached his child with fear and curiosity. Its eyes bore deep into his as it reached for him. The cries reverberated in his soul evoking a mixture of intense disgust and empathy; he succumbed to the latter. He grabbed a delivery blanket and draped it over the creature. Tears ran down his face.

"Shhh, shhh."

The infant's cries subsided once its eyes were shielded from the light. He placed the child between Susannah's thighs and took a step back as the illuminated eyes of the child stared back at him through the narrow opening in the blanket.

Susannah's energy had been depleted. She lay immobile moving her head dreamily from side to side; beads of perspiration raced down her forehead. She mumbled Craig's name then succumbed to exhaustion. Her waxen skin made her appear as if she had been thawed out.

Craig stumbled over to Barnaby and placed a hand on his back. Barnaby flinched. Craig took a deep breath and wiped his face while gently squeezing Barnaby's shoulder.

"I need a favor."

Barnaby grabbed a towel and rubbed his cadaverous face vigorously.

"No one must know about this." Craig shot a steely look at his friend. He looked at his family. Soft lamentations came from the thing that stirred underneath the covers. "Susannah must never know." He sighed wearily. "Help me get my child out of here. Can you do that for me?" He tightened his grip on Barnaby's shoulder as the metal in his eyes grew colder. "Can you help me? Please."

"How?" Barnaby's voice cracked.

"Put it to sleep. Give it a sedative, and I'll take it out of here."

"What about her?" Barnaby gestured toward Susannah.

"She doesn't have to know." Craig surveyed the empty room. "No one has to know. We already have a body." He cocked his head in the direction of the corpse. "You're in charge, document it as such." The iron in his stare weighed Barnaby down.

"But," Barnaby began, "I can't do this." He looked at Susannah. "It's not right."

"Barnaby, look at it." He pointed at the bundle of blanket in between Susannah's legs. "*That* is not human. That thing will cause her more pain than the dead one."

"Then let's get rid of it," Barnaby stated nervously.

Craig searched for answers. One child was dead, one *thing* was alive. A long healing process awaited Susannah once they buried their real daughter; presenting her with the creature that lay within the blanket would send her over the edge. Yet that was his child. He could deny its existence, but there was no denying that it was his blood that coursed through the creature's veins. What kind of life would it have other than become some experiment or a spectacle at a freak show? No. He would not allow his daughter to become some kind of laboratory rat, much less a caged attraction. Susannah's nightmare would never end.

"Please," Craig cried. "Just help me take my daughter out of here. Nobody has to know." He made a fist and pressed it to his chest. "Help me."

Barnaby caved in and administered the creature a mild sedative. Within seconds, it was fast asleep. They straightened out the equipment and made sure Susannah was okay before executing their plan. Barnaby took Craig and his daughter to an unoccupied room in a wing of the hospital that was sealed off for repairs while he filled out the death certificate at the nurse's station. Under Manner of Death, he wrote "Strangulation by umbilical cord," and under Cause of Death, he placed a checkmark in the box labeled Natural. He signed it and waited for the removal of the body. Several doctors approached him offering their support. He thanked them.

12:17 a.m.

Barnaby disguised Craig as an orderly and sent him out with "dirty linen" in a cart that was to be taken directly to the basement. Neither men spoke as they descended in the elevator. He slipped Craig through the loading docks at the back of the hospital. The guard on duty smiled and waved as he buzzed Barnaby and Craig by the door: hospital personnel often exited through the rear since the staff parking lot was located right there. He resumed his game of solitaire and took a bite of his tuna sandwich. The bundle of linen under Craig's arm stirred.

"Where did you park?" Barnaby bumped into Craig while looking over his shoulder, flinching at every car door that slammed. He avoided two men engaged in conversation that walked by him and nodded.

"On the other side just past that construction trailer over there."

Barnaby quickened his pace and hurried Craig on.

"Get my keys." Craig motioned to his pocket.

Barnaby reached into Craig's pocket while avoiding contact with the blanket. He opened the door, and Craig placed the bundle of linen in the backseat. Craig went to the driver's side door, stopped, and stared at Barnaby. "Thank you." The two regarded each other in silence before Craig rubbed his face and took a deep breath. "Thank you." He waved and got in. The tail lights disappeared around the corner.

"Dear God. What have I done?" Barnaby closed his eyes.

July 15, 1995, 8:40 a.m.

The following morning, Susannah awoke to the bad news and had to be heavily sedated. Craig exchanged looks with Barnaby and squeezed his wife's hands as she sobbed when several bouquets of flowers were delivered by friends and family that had not learned of their misfortune. He remained with her in the hospital for the next two days and notified the nurses' station that no more flowers were to be delivered. Finally, after the swelling of her womb subsided, she was released. Barnaby stared at the couple from the window as they exited the parking lot and crossed himself.

The first couple of months were hell on Susannah. She took a leave of absence from work and paced the house aimlessly. Dishes piled up, the stack of dirty clothes bred on a daily basis, a thin sheet of dust had settled over the television screen, and the mail often remained unopened on the kitchen table. Craig made several attempts to strike up conversations and watch movies to no avail. She would give him a blank stare accompanied by a dim smile. He distanced himself for a couple of weeks and allowed her to sort matters out while he attended to their newborn at the tree house.

THE HUNGER

Other men live to eat, while I eat to live.
—Socrates (quoted by Diogenes Laertius)

September 23, 2000

CRAIG COULD BARELY keep up with Athena's voracious appetite. She grew like a normal child over a span of three years, but her strength was uncanny. He would often find himself tumbling backward from one swipe of Athena's powerful arms, knowing well that she was merely playing. Besides her strength, her diet had changed dramatically as the beast within gradually surfaced. Baby food, cereal, bread, fruits, and chicken no longer satiated her incessant hunger. Now there came the craving for meat, a cornucopia that covered everything from beef to cold cuts to hot dogs whether raw or cooked. Craig had accepted the sudden change in her diet as part of evolution and struggled to keep up with her needs on a regular basis. Along with the never-ending demand for meat came a higher grocery bill, which he kept hidden from Susannah by putting in several hours of overtime to keep up with the expenses.

In the beginning, Craig had fed Athena out of pity, often wondering whether having taken her out of the hospital that night had been a monumental mistake. At times, he could not bear to look upon his child, recoiling in disgust and apathy every time she sought his love. She would sense the disdain as well and keep her distance. Only moral obligation coupled with parental instincts kept him coming back.

Physical contact with the creature was virtually absent during the first year. He would toss the food at her feet and walk away. For water, he would bring a small pot, scoop from the nearby stream, and place it to her lips without so much as touching or looking at her. At times the water ran down her chin onto her hairy, flaccid breasts. One time her hand came into contact with his as she attempted to grab the pot by the handle. He recoiled as if having grabbed a branding iron by the wrong end and dropped the pan. She too had been alarmed and sprang back defensively. He openly cursed his existence and the creature's, sending the pot across the field with his foot. Athena had run back to the tree and climbed in desperation. A pair of yellow gleaming eyes stared down at Craig then disappeared inside the tree house.

"Suit yourself," he commented into the night. As he walked away, he heard soft wails, stopped, and looked up at the tree house: a tear escaped.

Craig returned two days later with a bucket of fried chicken and biscuits he had picked up on the way home.

"Athena," he called out, "come get your food," and then in a whisper, "Daddy is here." There was no response. "Athena," he called, this time a bit louder. "I said come here right now." There was movement in the tree house. Athena descended slowly and, when she reached the bottom, remained crouched at the base of the tree.

"Come get your food." Craig waved the bucket.

She did not move.

"Athena, you get over here right now." He pointed to the ground at his feet.

She approached her father in calculated movements, sat on her canine hindquarters with her arms to her chest, and stared at the ground.

"I got you some food." He leaned over just far enough to lob the bucket of chicken in front of her. It fell on its side spilling some of the chicken and biscuits on the dirt. Athena looked away.

"What's wrong? Eat." He kicked the dirt-covered drumstick closer to her. "Eat."

She looked at the bucket and toyed with it. A black claw-like fingernail pushed the drumstick away.

"Listen, I haven't got all night. If you want to eat, that's fine. If not, then that's fine too." He cursed and turned to leave. "Whatever possessed God in heaven to have created you."

Athena let out a deep, painful groan. Craig turned and took in the slumping figure with her head drooping: she had pushed the bucket to the side.

"What? What is it? What the fuck do you want from me!?" He pointed at the bucket. "Eat your damned food."

The moaning continued.

"Listen, I really don't have time for this shit." He checked the luminescent markings on his watch. "Eat your damn food."

Athena whined like an injured dog.

"What's wrong now?" Craig frowned.

The clamoring escalated.

"Shh!" He looked over his shoulder. "Dammit. Somebody might hear you." He stepped closer. "Shut the fuck up," he said through clenched teeth and balled fists.

What happened next melted away whatever repugnance, disdain, and anger within him. His daughter reached for him like a toddler. The gesture rooted him to the ground and his knees shook as his legs began to fold. Whatever he had wanted to say came out as a series of guttural sounds as he dragged himself across the ground toward his daughter. Her whining turned into a soft whimper.

She sniffed and licked his hand while he caressed her disfigured head. She nuzzled against his chest, running her hot, coarse tongue across his chin and neck. Craig hugged his daughter for the first time. He could feel the strong, rapid breathing of her heart matching beats with his.

"I'm so sorry," he managed to say through tears and coughing.

She licked his face.

"Don't you worry about anything. Daddy's not going to let anything happen to you." He hugged her tighter. "Daddy loves you very much."

That night the relationship between father and daughter had been forged. Pity turned into unrestrained love, disgust into acceptance. He now looked forward to spending time with his child. They would sit and dine together under the tree house, sometimes up in the tree house when it was either raining or snowing. He would ask her how her day had gone, and she would respond with a series of snorts and grunts. Recently, he had bought her some Dr. Seuss books in an attempt to teach her how to read. Although she appeared to be soaking in the words, her interest lay in the colorful pictures and the sound of her father's voice as he read to her under the mysterious light from a cylindrical object. Once she fell asleep, he would tuck her in, kiss her wrinkled forehead, climb down, and return home with a smile.

As months passed, the filial bond between father and daughter grew. Where there was once a monster now stood a daughter. Where there was once ugliness now stood acceptance and savage beauty. The more time they shared, the more he accepted his role within her world. He could now stand before the creature and look past the demonic disguise to embrace the loving soul of his true daughter. At times, he saw it as a test from God. And if indeed the Almighty had cast down a curse upon him by tainting the flesh of his flesh with abominable features, then he had passed it like Lazarus with flying colors. Nothing more than a litmus test.

AL BRUNO

At the beginning, keeping the secret from Susannah was quite a chore. The initial strain had distanced the couple as he would break down into tirades that resulted in excessive cursing with objects and doors being either slammed in the house or launched in the garage. She often kept her distance from him in the mornings when he was at his worst.

"Craig," she would begin, "are you getting enough sleep?" This would immediately be followed by either a silent response that conveyed indifference as he grabbed his coffee and walked away or a "What the fuck does it matter?" followed by an occasional "Who gives a fuck!" After a handful of these early-morning greetings, she avoided him altogether. She would brew coffee, set his cup on the table, and retreat into a corner of the sofa, sometimes into the guest bedroom to watch the news. Craig would sit at the kitchen counter sipping and yawning. At times, he would fall asleep on the counter, and Susannah would approach stealthily, tap him on the shoulder, and whisper his name with such delicacy as one would say blessings to a newborn. "You're going to be late for work." He would stare at her and frown, then watch as she smiled and walked away.

The only comfort Susannah found was having the house to herself for about an hour before he arrived. And when he called and said that he had some work that had to be done before the next day, she would rejoice; another two to three hours of freedom, sometimes more. This allowed her the opportunity to unwind: get on the treadmill, watch some television, take a nice hot bath with a glass of wine while listening to some Pink Floyd, and catch up on some crossword puzzles. By the time he got home, she would be fast asleep. His dinner would be waiting in the microwave, which often remained untouched.

Susannah never once questioned Craig's sporadic mood changes. They had begun when they returned from the hospital from that "tragic" night. She had gone through a period of withdrawal that was expected and quite normal. And although Craig rarely discussed it, she concluded that he had been profoundly affected by that night. She remembered how he was constantly conducting inventory of the travel bag when the *time* would come. How he took over cleaning the house, washing the dishes, and doing the laundry, not wanting her to lift anything heavier than a slipper. Finally, how he had transformed the guest bedroom into the baby's room. The walls had remained white. They had refused an ultrasound and merely prayed for a healthy child, wanting the sex of the child to remain a surprise and then settle on the color after the birth, yet the surprise they got was not the one they had expected.

With Craig going through his own trials and tribulations, as she figured, it was best to give him as much time as necessary in order to let him regroup himself. Their marriage had been placed on hold. She didn't even bother to question his late-night disappearance acts. Initially, she immediately suspected an affair. But when both of their cars were still in the driveway, she got a bit curious, searched the house, and discovered the porch door and the back gate unlocked. She had waited silently in the dark on several occasions, often nodding off, to be awakened by the sound of the back gate opening as Craig sauntered dreamily across the backyard. "Where have you been?" she had asked one night, not revealing that she had been keeping surveillance of his after-midnight rendezvous for quite some time. He had been startled but recovered quickly and responded with a lackadaisical, "Out for a walk." *Every night?* And every morning, she would inspect his shirts for foreign perfumes and lipstick, and when asleep, she would inspect his back for scratchmarks. Nothing. Only the foul smell of wet dog and the forest. Several months later, his wanderings lessened to three maybe four times a week. Once her investigations had turned up nothing, she had accepted it as part of Craig's "therapeutic readjustment period." People dealt with tragic events in their lives in different ways: Craig's healing process comprised of seemingly harmless walks in the woods at the darkest hours of the night. It had become an acceptable routine. Until, that is, he came home with a set of gashes across his shoulder. She had asked him about the marks. "Oh, these. I must've gotten them when I brushed up against the rake the other day." Again she checked for female fragrance but came up empty. And although she had never bought into his story, he had been so trustworthy that she forced herself to believe that indeed he had been injured in the toolshed. If there was one thing Susannah was sure of, whatever Craig was doing in the forest, it did not involve another human being.

December 24, 2000, 11:55 p.m.

The drive home was quiet. Craig looked through the corner of his eye and thumbed the steering wheel as he searched for something to say to his wife who was absorbed gazing into the trees as the car negotiated the road. The headlights cast an unearthly glow that breached the skirt of the forest and was rapidly swallowed by the darkness. Lane markers cut through the middle of the road like white-hot embers that disappeared under the car. Only Bing Crosby's voice echoed inside the car as he sang "Silver Bells."

They were returning from the house of Susannah's coworker. It had been a small gathering of selected friends and family. The hosts were adamant vegans and had opted to furnish the tables with celery and blue cheese, steamed broccoli, various assortments of sushi rolls, and salads containing romaine lettuce and spinach, among other dishes. Craig had found this amusing.

"What about shrimp cocktails?" he had whispered to Susannah.

"They don't eat bottom dwellers."

"Right." He piled more celery sticks on his plate.

The hosts were absolutely delightful, and Craig admitted that he was having a pretty nice time. Adults karaoked and shared childhood memories and toasted while the kids raced back and forth: some of the boys were outside having a snowball fight while the girls retreated to a room to play with the dollhouses and watch music videos. The gathering appeared to have been set up by Albert Kincaid himself. The hammer fell when the kids were ordered to gather in the living room to receive their gifts. Because it was still Christmas Eve, each kid was allowed to open only one present; the rest would have to wait until tomorrow.

The children gathered in a semicircle in the middle of the living room, nudging each other and laughing as their names were called out to receive a gift. "Cool!" one of the boys had yelled as he tore the wrapping paper like a hyena tearing flesh off a wildebeest and found the picture of a telescope on the box. "Can we look at the stars now?" he had pleaded. "Tomorrow, I promise you," his father reassured him. After the third gift was handed out, Craig caught sight of his wife lost in thought as a painful smirk draped itself across her face. Her eyes were fixated on the children. Craig watched as she slowly backed away from the crowd to wipe away the tears, placed her drink on the table, and disappeared stealthily into the bathroom with a hand cupping her mouth. Suddenly, the festive warmth ran from his body as if the window had been thrust open to allow the winter air inside. Susannah had remained in the bathroom for over ten minutes; only Craig noticed her absence. He sighed heavily and forced a multitude of pretentious smiles with hollow laughter. Soon thereafter, after Susannah emerged from the bathroom with puffy eyes as the last gifts were exchanged, they left.

"I think Susy has had one too many," the hostess smiled.

"Yeah, I think you're right," Craig fired back.

Embraces and "Thank-you's" were exchanged at the door. And as they walked down the driveway, Susannah closed her eyes and relished the cold of the night pressing against her skin.

"Hope you had a good time," she pressed her head against his shoulder.

"Yeah, I had a great time," he responded while forcing a smile. Those were the last words spoken until they got home.

December 25, 2000, 1:03 a.m.

Susannah closed her eyes as Craig ran his hands through her hair, staring at the flickering glows of red, blue, and green lights as they bounced off her silhouette. Her raven hair melted with the dark background, giving her a ghostly appearance. He reached her neck and massaged it gently. She sipped her wine, brushed her hair to the side, and craned her neck. He sipped his beer and gazed into the blinking rainbow of lights from the Christmas tree. He had volunteered to throw a couple of logs in the fireplace; she declined and decided they get a blanket, stare at the tree in silence, and surrender themselves to wine and beer. He then suggested they each open one present, but when she declined, he refrained from further conversation, kept massaging her neck, and drank, staring at the soft, hypnotic glow of the assortment of lights as they carved an intermittent constellation in the dark. Thirty minutes later, he gently slid her snoring head off his chest and onto a sofa cushion.

"Merry Christmas, Susannah," he whispered while securing the blanket around her feet and tucking it around her head. "I love you." A gentle finger traced her face followed by an even gentler kiss on the lips.

Craig navigated his way around the house like a thief. He grabbed his jacket, shoved the house keys into his pocket, and left quietly out the porch door. An uninvited gust of wind and flurries pushed past him and made its way to Susannah. She stirred and curled into a deeper fetal position. He adjusted his collar and stepped onto the snow-covered porch, trekking his way to the side of the garage. Ice cracked and fell from the hinges as he gave the side door several tugs. The fluorescent lights hummed and buzzed as they struggled to shake off the cold. Craig rubbed his hands vigorously as he stepped over an oil pan. With a final buzz, the garage was fully lit. He raised the trunk of his '72 Ford Mustang and opened a box decorated with yellow and black quarts of oil. A smile spread across his face like thin ice cracking underneath a skater's weight as he gently took out Athena's gift. He couldn't wait to see the look on her face as she tore open the box and pulled out a Raggedy Ann doll. It was time to discard the mutilated teddy bear that he had bought her last Christmas. Prior to this, she had been content to play with basketballs, footballs, and even some letter blocks that she gnawed on rather than spell out words. When she had received the teddy bear, she merely stared at it, turning it over and over. Then something wonderful happened: she cradled it in her arms and began rocking back and forth. Where had she learned this behavior? Maternal instinct? The thought of Athena bearing children raised every hair on his body. Could she have children? Normal children? Or would she give birth to a horde of little demons? He shuddered and left the garage cradling the box underneath his left arm, glancing over at the porch before exiting through the gate in the backyard and vanishing into the woods.

Although he had navigated his way to Athena's house without the aid of either a compass or flashlight hundreds of times thus having carved out a path both in his mind and through the forest, the journey proved trickier when it either rained or snowed. Foggy glasses, gales whipping tree limbs into swordfights, mud puddles, and snow converted the route into an obstacle course. Tonight, snow and winds joined forces to produce one of these challenging expeditions.

The trees began to thin out as the clearing came into view. The stream had frozen solid, and Craig nearly fell as he attempted to jump over it. The gift fell. He picked it up and wiped off the snow. The wind was more prominent in the clearing, forcing him to shield his eyes. Snow had accumulated on the roof and left side of the tree house, leaving the right side exposed. Craig had weatherproofed the outside, insulated the entire inside with thick fiberglass insulation, and provided Athena with thick quilts which were replaced every month. From up close, it could easily be passed over to an untrained eye. From a distance, it stood out like an inkblot on a sheet of white paper during the winter. This concerned Craig a great deal. What if someone discovers the tree house and decides to take a peek? Some kids out playing hide-and-seek? How would Athena react? So far, no one had ventured into this section of the forest. And if they had, then the tree house had remained obscure. He often wondered who had been the architect of the tree house.

Craig approached the foot of the tree and took a deep breath to call out his daughter then decided otherwise; it would ruin the surprise. He reached over and pulled on a cord that released a rope ladder. Athena, of course, did not require the use of the ladder. He often marveled at the dexterity and speed with which she maneuvered up and down the tree. Her movements comprised of a synthesis of feline gracefulness with the agility of a monkey.

Climbing with the package proved cumbersome as he scaled the ladder with one hand. He reached a small clearance underneath the tree house of about two feet where the floor had been carefully secured against three thick branches that extended outward. He placed the package on the crook of the branches and touched something gelatinous. It was some sort of thick, viscous liquid. Craig secured an arm around the ladder and reached into his pocket for a pen flashlight. He switched it on, placed it between his teeth, and raised his fingers. Blood. Athena! Something had happened to her.

"Athena . . ." The flashlight fell to the ground and was swallowed by the snow. He punched through the bottom of the door and pulled himself up, kicking his feet to propel himself upward.

"Athena?"

Something scrambled in a corner and let out a wolf's growl.

"Athena? Are you okay?" He extended his hands and probed the wall for the emergency flashlight. The light flickered as he pressed the button, giving it a whack on his hand before steadying. More blood. He aimed the light at the crimson trail and followed it as it culminated into a large pool at Athena's feet.

She growled.

The beam of light shook as he traced her body. Blood-soaked hands held the carcass of an animal while she sank her teeth into its flesh and ripped off chunks of meat. Her pupils shrank when he brought the light to her face; her mouth was covered in blood. She grinned and offered the prize to her father, revealing bloodied canine teeth with shards of flesh hanging in between them.

Craig turned away. He lowered the flashlight and caught sight of a dog's head to his right. One of the eyes had been bitten out, and the tongue rolled out of its mouth in a mocking gesture. The flashlight fell from his hands; the ray of light came to rest on Athena as she fed. He could hear the flesh being ripped from the carcass and the smacking of her gums. He sat back against the wall and covered his face with his hands while snow gathered on Athena's gift . . . .

Thus began Craig's penance. He had returned home with an upset stomach—stopping every so often when vile rushed up his throat—and poured himself several drinks recapping the events at the tree house. Perhaps it had been an isolated incident; it would never happen again. Had he forgotten to feed her? It had been a day since he last saw her. He made it a point to bring her enough food to last for two days at a time, but her appetite did appear to be growing substantially over the past several months. He poured himself another drink. He would visit her tomorrow and explain to her that what she had done was unacceptable. Would she understand? Sometimes when he spoke to her it felt as if he was attempting to communicate with a dog. She did understand simple commands such as "Come here," "Sit down," "Place your head on Daddy's lap," and "Stop," but how could he expect her to rationalize last night's actions? He feared that, although Athena shared human characteristics, the beast within was much stronger, and attempting to suppress her primordial side was going to prove a daunting task, if not downright impossible.

Over the next two weeks, Athena resumed to eating only what her father brought her, and he had dismissed the entire incident as a one-time spur of the moment "evolutionary detour." That changed, of course, when he began to discover the skulls and bones of more dogs in the tree house. He had had to cover his nose at the smell of dried blood, feces, and urine that permeated throughout the tree house, which he feverishly attempted to cleanse and mask with pine-scented cleaners and air fresheners to no avail. Bathing her in the winter had also become quite a chore. Maintaining his daughter and her home clean had become a full-time job.

With time, the remains of animals, although discomforting, became a routine that no longer bothered him. He would bring bags and a shovel with him to dispose of "Athena's leftovers" about a hundred yards out. And just when Craig had adjusted to her new staple of food, she surprised him once again. Approximately two months after her first kill, Athena sought larger prey. The gnawed skull of a deer attached to a severed spinal chord greeted him as he came to pick up bones one night. He had opened his mouth to reprimand her, but the sight of Athena extracting a set of intestines from a gaping hole on the carcass of the deer and tearing into them like a child tearing open a bag of goodies left him voiceless. Craig sat back and watched his daughter eat. The disgust that he initially experienced turned into amazement. There wasn't any real crime that had been committed here; she was eating to survive—nothing more, nothing less. What troubled Craig the most was not her carnivorous activities, but the brutal reality that, as much as he wished, as much as he prayed, as much as he hoped, his daughter would never walk among society. Whatever human characteristics she shared with her parents were a satirical visage to what really lay at the core of her being. And with each kill, his daughter's humanity waned while the creature within progressively clawed its way to the surface. The only comfort Craig felt was in Athena acknowledging him. Their bond was unflappable . . . for now. What if someday something would snap inside of her? Would he be able to control her? Would she turn against him? Craig leaned against the wall and smiled as Athena enjoyed her meal. She smiled back. Craig shivered from the cold and the diabolic smile that exposed reddened teeth.

hunt-ing [noun]: sport of pursuing and killing wild game animals in order to provide food, or simply for the thrill of the chase, or for the enjoyment of outdoor life.

August 20, 2005, 9:07 a.m.

*B*E STILL. BE *quiet. Don't move a muscle. They're coming.*
Snap!

Ted glued himself to the tree, clutched the rifle closer to his chest, and tightened his grip, trigger finger twitching. Another twig snapped. He swallowed hard and struggled desperately to relax or risk giving away his position from the pounding in his chest. Leaning ever so slowly, he peeked around the tree like a lion hunting gazelles through tall grass and spotted his victim. A triumphant grin spread across his face: his first kill.

The hunter crouched and waited for a shot. His body became rigid when the unsuspecting target turned in his direction. The blood in his veins traveled like light in a fiber-optic cable. The prey stared right at him: Ted stared back. Olive drab, brown, and forest-green face paint; a forest camouflage uniform; jungle boots; a camouflage beanie; and lines of black shoe polish on his hands—the ultimate killing machine.

The prey scanned the area, took a couple of steps, and stopped. Assuring itself that there was no threat, it proceeded forward.

The safety was clicked off as the weapon was raised. Aligning the front and back sights, Ted exhaled and squeezed the trigger.

Foompf! Foompf!

The victim staggered back and looked down at the two red blotches on his side. One of the rounds had struck him on the hip.

"Shit!" He staggered and braced himself against a tree.

"Yeah!" Ted jumped and pumped his fist in the air. "Gotcha, Karl." He reached for his radio. "I gotta call this in."

Karl slung the weapon on his shoulder and wiped the red paint with leaves. The game was over for him while Ted's would continue. He leaned against a tree and crossed his arms. Besides being caught, his team had only scored two kills while Ted's was up to five. Each of the members on the losing team would have to buy a PlayStation 2 game for one member of the winning team, and they got to choose the games they wanted, which meant that his team could fork over up to $50 for a game. More frustrating than the taunts was the fact that this had all been his idea. He was the one who had upped the stakes and promised to personally deliver a victory if it meant that he would be the last man standing. And now he had just become the fifth casualty. That meant that it was up to the last two guys, or else they'd have to hand over their allowances to Ted's team. There was still hope.

"Yes!"

Karl watched as Ted raised his rifle and pumped it in the air.

"Hey, Karl," Ted yelled. "Guess what? Tim just whacked your brother, and Chuck is running for his life. They got 'im cornered and he's outta ammo." He laughed. "Get ready to pay up, buddy." He took off like a deer jumping over fallen branches and zigzagged through the trees.

All hope evaporated. *Great*. It was over. Chuck was the last one left, and with his asthma, there was no way he was going to outrun the posse. His mind went back to last year when they found Chuck through the wheezing noises he was making from behind a bush; he had been on the verge of an asthma attack. Although Karl hated getting stuck with Chuck every time, he tolerated it because Chuck's father had a deep wallet: he supplied the entire team with paintball ammunition, CO_2 cartridges, and even paid for the hour they spent on the course. Not bad, but losing sucked.

Karl pushed himself from the tree and opted for a shortcut through the creek that ran adjacent to the park. The creek had been placed off limits after Ted's cousin tore his knee wide open on a jagged rock last year when they had lost yet again. It took eighty-seven stitches and a whole lot of apologizing from the manager who was ordered by the owner to pick up the tab in order to keep the parents from suing. A majority of the boys were pissed because splashing through the water added "realism" and a Ramboesque scenario to the entire course. One kid had even tried to cover himself in mud from the banks and reenact the mud scene but had to strip and bathe in the stream after the mud turned out to be animal droppings.

Karl walked alongside the stream, picking up rocks and skipping them on the water. Properly thrown, a good oval-shaped, flat rock with a bit of girth to it could give up to five skips. He had done it only once and won a Mike Piazza rookie card from Ted. He remembered Ted's face as the stone took its fifth bounce. When they returned home, Ted took a long last look at the card before placing it in Karl's hands. Karl had smiled as he showed Ted his new baseball card. "Thanks, buddy. Nice doing business with you."

Today, however, it was Ted's turn to enjoy the spoils of war.

"Aw, the hell with it." Karl came across the perfect stone. It was smooth, superbly rounded at the edges, about half an inch in width, and just big enough to fit comfortably between his index finger, thumb, and middle finger. He wiped the stone on his pants and placed the rifle on the ground. Stepping forward with his left foot, he brought his arm to waist level, took a deep breath before exhaling, and flicked the stone across the widest part of the stream.

One . . . two . . . three . . . four . . . five . . . six.

"Wow!" Karl searched for an audience. "Damn. I gotta get that stone back. I'll get one of Derek Jeter's rookie cards from Ted. At least a game with it."

He grabbed the gun by the sling and jumped into the stream. The water reached his knees and gradually rose to his thighs. A couple of steps further, it was up to his waist. He stopped and eyeballed the distance to the other side—about ten feet. Raising the gun over his head, he took a tentative step. His foot landed on a large rock and, when he took another step, lost his footing and slipped under, gulping two hearty mouthfuls of water. He flailed his arms and kicked his feet frantically before planting his feet and pushing off, breaking the surface like a seal.

Karl heaved as water flew from his nose and mouth in jets. Coughing violently, he dragged his soaking body to the bank where he threw up. He looked back and watched as his paintball gun traveled down the stream.

"Shit!"

He ran parallel to the stream dodging rocks and branches that extended to the shore. Up ahead about twenty feet, the gun disappeared around a bend.

"No!" He picked up speed. An entire summer's earnings of mowing lawns and cleaning up driveways were on the verge of disappearing down the stream that fed into the reservoir. Breathing heavy and pounding the ground as fast as he could, Karl raced to the gun's rescue. As he made the turn, his left foot caught a branch that reached into the water, slingshooting him airborne a good five feet onto the pebble-draped banks. His face crashed into the water.

"Ugh." Karl pushed himself up brushing mud and small rocks from his hands and face. He looked back and saw the gun resting against a tree trunk.

"Whew!" He swiped at the flies as he walked and covered his nose, stopped short of the gun and leaned over. "Oh shit!"

The tree trunk turned out to be half a torso with an arm that had been torn off just below the elbow. Innards—missing. Legs—missing. Right arm—missing. The head—missing. What flesh remained on the neck hung like a deflated balloon. Karl searched for a long stick to use as a pointer. He probed the mutilated torso and felt vile sprinting up his esophagus as thousands of maggots spilled onto the ground like a torn bag of rice. Hundreds of flies assaulted him. Suddenly, the entire surroundings seemed to have silenced as a monsoon of dread slammed against his body. Stepping into the water with shaky legs, he snatched the gun, raced across a shallow section of the stream like a wildebeest, and kicked up dirt and leaves as he sped through the trees like a rabbit evading a fox.

Back at the brook, the flies went back to their business of laying eggs on the carcass . . .

AL BRUNO

THE HIGH SCHOOL REUNION

Most friendship is feigning, most loving mere folly.
—Shakespeare, *As You Like It, II, 7*

June 29, 2009, 6:17 p.m.

THE YOUNG MAN in the picture sported a voluminous head of disheveled hair that had earned him the nickname Helmethead. Crooked glasses, crooked necktie, and a crooked smile had made him one of the least likely candidates to succeed in life, much less marry one of the most sought-after girls in the graduating class. Yet behind all the incongruence in his façade, there lay a hidden enigmatic personality, perseverance, and charisma that rendered him appealing. And once the man inside surfaced, shed the glasses for contact lenses, and straightened out his tie, there remained little—if any—resemblance between the boy in the picture and the man holding the yearbook.

Craig ran a hand over his picture. He flipped through the pages to Susannah's picture, tracing her jet-black hair with his finger and following the contour of her lips, the delicate silkiness of her skin. He closed his eyes and inhaled, returning to the sweet smell of vanilla-scented shampoo as he stood behind her while they waited for the photographer to take their yearbook pictures. He read the words below her photograph.

To Craig, a smart, caring, and wonderful friend. Thanks for all the laughs and helping me with the SATs. See ya in college!

Love, Suzy-Q

He smiled and flipped the pages. With the exception of over a dozen teachers and members of the debating team, math, and bowling team, Craig's yearbook was void of any other entries. Susannah's, on the other hand, was full of so many signings that a majority of the faces could not be distinguished. He closed the yearbook and tossed it beside the four shirts and seven ties on the bed.

"Did you pick up the dress?" Susannah walked into the bedroom, drying her hair with a towel.

"And this." Craig waved the dress in front of her while taking in her nakedness and picked up a bottle of red wine from the side of the bed.

"What's that for? I'm sure there's going to be plenty to drink."

"Not for the reunion, for us."

"Oh," she smiled.

"Why wait until later?" He pressed against her body and placed his hands around her waist.

"Not now." Susannah pushed him off gently. "Save it for later." She grabbed his wrist and pulled back on the sleeve to look at his watch. "I don't want to be late."

Craig watched as she walked away and stood before the mirror ruffling her hair with the towel. She reached into one of the drawers, pulled out the hair blower, and caught his reflection. "Hey, you perv." She smiled and switched off the blower. "You okay?"

"Uh, yeah. I . . . don't know which shirt to wear." He sighed and looked helplessly at the four shirts without really seeing any of them.

"Let's see." Susannah placed the blower on the dresser and approached the bed. She contemplated the shirts and pointed at the light-blue, sea-foam colored one. "That one." To the side of the shirt lay the yearbook. "What's this?" She climbed onto the bed and grabbed it, flipped through the pages, and stopped at the photographs of the cheerleading squad. "Wow. I wonder if any of the girls will be there." She pointed at several faces while calling out their names. "Sally, there's Barbara . . . uh . . . I think this is Joanne . . . or was it Dianne? Here's Alison." A couple of pages over were pictures of the football, baseball, and wrestling teams. "And the guys."

Craig's heart fussed as she skimmed the photographs in silence.

"My god." She closed the book and looked at him. "I can't believe it's been twenty years. Seems like yesterday." She paused and sighed. "Where have the years gone?"

"I don't know." Craig bit his lip and shook his head. "But I do know this . . ." He crawled onto the bed on his knees and reached for her hands. "I'm still here. I always have been." He kissed her on the forehead. "And I will always be."

"I love you," she whispered in his ear while stroking the back of his neck.

Craig caught their reflection. He watched as his hands gently traced her back, reaching down and caressing her buttocks.

"Hey." She slapped him playfully on the shoulder.

AL BRUNO

Craig and his reflection locked eyes. The image began to swirl until Athena's face manifested itself in the mirror. She had her mother's eyes. Her powerful jaws opened, revealing a collection of menacing serrated teeth. Craig smiled. "I love you." He winked.

"And I love you too," Susannah replied as she separated herself and held his face in her hands. She kissed him and got off the bed. "But we're going to be late."

Athena watched as her mother walked toward her; their faces met and forged into one, leaving only Susannah's, who switched on the blower and resumed drying her hair.

Oh, Susy! I'm sorry. Will you forgive me? If only I could tell you. Perhaps one day . . .

8:23 p.m.

Susannah had been blabbering about the good times in high school throughout the entire ride. Craig could not conjure up any really good times except for those spent with Susannah. For him, life began the moment they met. As they neared the school, a cornucopia of memories began to unfold in his mind. Some were fond, but most were lackluster. Other than having his name engraved on plaques for Excellent Attendance, Dean's Honor Roll, and Math Club, he was virtually a ghost in the annals of the school's history. Regional and state championship banners, trophies, and other awards for athletic achievements were the cornerstones of their school: a place where hometown heroes are forever enshrined.

Craig made a right on Cedar Lane following the winding road about a quarter of a mile where it divided into two lanes; he stayed on the right and slowed down when he came upon a caravan of taillights. Looming on the horizon like the Acropolis amid a collection of orange, blue, and white spotlights representing the school colors fencing in the sky lay Fairfield High School. Three cars ahead, there was a sign with blinking Christmas lights on its borders greeting the members of the graduating class of 1989.

"Wow!" Susannah squeezed Craig's thigh and placed a hand on her chest. "I can't believe we're really here." She leaned over and placed her head on his shoulder.

"Yep. We're here." Craig draped his arm around his wife. Half of him was excited; the other half was experiencing a suffocating premonition urging him to do a U-turn and head back home. It would be nice to reunite with some of his friends like Jeromy, Liam, CJ from the math club, and

Jimmy Sullivan from the chemistry club. He had lost contact with them over eight years ago.

On the other hand, the thought of being around Susannah's circle of friends brought only migraines. The world from which she had come from was an alien planet to him. The taunting, weird looks, and snide remarks he received the times in which they were seen together during high school resurfaced and pressed against his chest like a rogue wave. His friends would bombard him with questions: "Man, how did you hook up with her? Have you slept with her?" and "Dude, does she have a sister?" Her friend's remarks were quite the contrary: "Girl, like, are you on drugs? Is this charity work?" and "Suzy, are you *that* horny?" He had decided that talking over the phone would keep the inquiries and gossip to a minimum. The irony of it all is that Susannah paid practically no attention to the rumors while he was more giddy and apprehensive. "Don't let it bother you," she would remark. And he would respond with, "Okay," knowing well that it was not. Craig had managed to erase these episodes from his mind. Tonight, as they reached the parking lot, the murky memories came knocking on the door of his mind. This time, they had company. Something about revisiting their alma mater seemed inappropriate if not downright dangerous.

"Honey!"

Craig mashed the brakes missing the couple in front of his bumper by inches. He put up an apologetic hand only to be answered with a flip of the bird by the girl and a "Watch it, asshole," from the guy.

"Hey," Susannah grabbed his arm. "Are you okay?"

"Yeah." He nodded. "Just a bit nervous, that's all."

"Me too." She massaged her hands. "Over there. There's a spot next to the white car."

Craig inched the car forward and parked. Susannah flipped down the sun visor and dug through her purse.

"Mind turning on the light for a second."

While she put the finishing touches on her face, Craig watched people getting out of their cars, making their way to the entrance. Women in evening dresses of all designs, lengths, and colors paraded before him like some makeshift parody of the Academy Awards. He scrutinized them from head to toe and wagered to himself that Susannah looked better than any of them, a bet he would later regret having even thought about.

Susannah turned to him, shoved a hand in her dress to adjust her breasts and transparent spaghetti strap, and smiled. "Do I look okay?"

"Wow! Let me get my gun. I'm gonna be fighting every man in there."

"I'm serious." She slapped him playfully on the arm.

"You look absolutely beautiful." He unbuckled his seatbelt and leaned toward her until his face was an inch from hers, lifted her chin, and kissed her softly. "I love you."

"I love you too." She caught sight of a group of people walking by and pushed herself away. "Ready?"

No, I'm not. Let's just go home, grab the yearbook and the bottle of wine, and when you're drunk enough, I'll tell you about your daughter, our daughter. You'd be very proud of her. "Yes. Let's get this over with."

As they entered the school, there was a group of about seven people pointing to poster boards with hundreds of high school pictures. They received their name tags at the door by current high school seniors who had volunteered for the event. Craig took in the handsome young man and his equally stunning, flawless, trophy-doll sidekick. *The joy of youth.* He particularly envied the soft yet rugged looks of the young man and wished he had had those same features in high school. To them, Craig was just another guest. He could've told them that he was the Joe Montana or Mickey Mantle of Fairfield High back in the days, and they would've bought it.

Susannah squeezed his hand nervously as they took the stairs to the gymnasium. "Thank you," she whispered while kissing him. They passed several people and smiled. She paused as they approached the entrance to the gym, placed a hand on her chest, exhaled nervously, patted her hair, checked her fingernails, realigned her bra straps, adjusted her panty line, and brushed her dress.

"How do I look?"

"Beautiful." He smiled. "Absolutely stunning." And she did. Perhaps too beautiful. Although he felt imperious accompanying Aphrodite, there was a bit of concern, not about her attire, which could have lured a ship into a sandbar like a lighthouse on a foggy night, but rather the multitude of testosterone-saturated vultures that lurked behind those doors. They seemed to follow her everywhere.

"Shall we?" Craig nodded toward the doors. She squeezed his hand and nodded. He pushed open the doors.

The gym had been divided into two halves: dining and dancing. The dining area was moderately lit with several rows of round tables, but a good portion of the crowd seemed more at home on the bleachers. The lights over the dancing area had been dimmed just enough to provide comfort. Two strobe lights and half a dozen orange, blue, and white spotlights were positioned just outside the perimeter.

Small clusters of people were scattered about engaged in conversations and laughter. At the far end of the gymnasium right above the bleachers was a banner with bold black letters—Welcome Back Class of '89. The backboards were covered with crepe paper and balloons. A couple of guys played with a balloon at one of the hoops. In between the other bleachers and the entrance to the men's locker room was the DJ. Four giant speakers were arranged at either sides of the audio equipment. The banquet tables were located at the other end of the gym underneath the scoreboard. They began to make their way toward the tables when a blonde woman in a black sequin dress approached them and stared at Susannah's name tag.

"Susannah? Suzy? Suzy Q? Is that you?"

"Sally?" Susannah raised her eyebrows. "OMG! You haven't changed a bit."

The women embraced. Craig watched as they twisted and turned in a circular dance.

"Girl, let me take a look at you," Sally said. She looked at Susannah from head to toe. "What have you been doing? You look fabulous. My oh my. Time has been very good to you."

Susannah placed a hand on Craig's arm. "Sally, this is my—"

"Hey, guys." Sally waved two other women and four cavemen over. "Look who's here, Suzy Q."

The women smiled as they strolled over. It didn't take Craig long to place the faces of the women to their younger selves in high school: Barbara Hunt, whose reputation for screwing jocks and supposedly the economics teacher had earned her the nickname of Hunt the Cunt; and Alison Thorn, a watered-down lapdog version of Sally Forrester. If Sally wore green eye shadow, so would Alison. If Sally wore a tight black miniskirt, Alison would see to it that hers was tighter and shorter. And if Sally said she had slept with the captain of the football team, Alison would do the entire team, including the water boy. Despite her incessant attempts, which Sally tolerated and was somewhat flattered by, Alison would remain in second place. Sally reveled in being the icon for Alison's obsession. Next came the men. The vultures stared at Susannah, exchanged comments, and began to make their descent. It was mating season. Craig stood like a prop in the background with both hands buried in his pockets, fiddling with the car keys. One of the men leaned over and said something to the tallest and burliest of the quartet. Craig's blood chilled as if he had been given liquid nitrogen in an IV: it was Jake Winthrop, the Fairfield High Piltdown man. He approached the women and literally devoured Susannah with his eyes.

While she had her back to the men, Jake leaned to one side and fixed his eyes on Susannah's ass. He turned to the other guy, Hugh Collins—captain of the lacrosse team—bit his lower lip, and grabbed his crotch.

"Suzy," Sally pointed at the four sacks of muscle. "You remember the guys, don't you? Charles Lance, Ted "Bundy" Wright, Hugh "Tom" Collins, and of course, Jake Winthrop. Jake was captain of the football team, remember?"

Susannah extended her hand. Jake spread his tentacles and reeled her in: an octopus prying open a clam. Slimy lips hunted Susannah's, but she subtly dodged them and smiled. He succeeded only in landing a suction cup on her cheek.

Craig's blood turned to magma.

She pushed away gingerly and turned to Craig. "Guys, this is my husband, Craig."

The men stared at Craig as if he were naked. Susannah used this distraction to break free from Jake's stronghold. She walked over to Craig and clasped onto him. Jake sneered like a shark as he sized up Craig.

"Oh, you're married," Sally smirked, looked at Craig, and cocked her head. "Craig? Craig Miller?" She placed a hand on her chest. "OMG! It is you." She gazed at Susannah in disbelief and suppressed a laugh. "Wow. I never would've guessed," she said, turning to the other women and rolling her eyes.

Craig's body tensed as the voice inside beckoned for a hasty retreat. But he remained poised, met the sardonic stares of the four men, and stood his ground. A gentle squeeze on his arm from his wife reminded him to remain calm. He shifted his weight and took a quick glance at the rest of the crowd before staring straight into Jake's ravenous eyes. A sinister smile slowly appeared on the Neanderthal's liquor-contorted face. The other three men turned their heads and chuckled.

"Come on, let's get another beer." Charles placed a hand on Jake's shoulder and led him away; Ted and Hugh followed high-fiving one another.

"Ahem. Well, uh, ladies, meet Susannah's husband, Craig Miller." Sally stepped aside as if introducing the next act at a three-ring circus. Each of the women rendered a diseased handshake accompanied by a plastic smile; Alison barely touched his hand. Pointless conversations, irrelevant issues of life, and a well-orchestrated façade that had been honed from over two decades of diligent practice consumed what Craig officially declared the most wretched ten minutes of his life. He squirmed in place and forced several laughs to avoid climbing the walls. The car keys represented freedom, but despite his inclinations to run out howling, he knew very well that this was Susannah's show. This is the world in which she had been conceived, the world where she had lived throughout high school, and no matter how much he loathed them, they were her friends. She spoke their language. To them, he was the intruder. As he listened to their gibberish and took a good look at his wife alongside the moronic trio, Craig indeed wondered how he had managed to land Susannah. Just when he thought things could not get any worse, the sharks circled in with beers in hand. Jake chewed on a drumstick and devoured it in one barbaric bite without so much as batting an eyelid at Craig.

Craig's palate went dry. Sweaty hands balled into fists in his pockets. Jake let out a thunderous burp and smiled, blowing into his face. Craig closed his eyes and swatted the air around him.

"OMG," Sally waved the air around her. "Dis-gus-ting. Totally."

The women took a couple of steps away and resumed their chatter while Craig was left to take on the scourge of Fairfield High and his Huns.

"So," Jake began his frontal assault. "*You* got Suzy?" He looked at Craig up and down and let out a snorted laugh. "She sure doesn't ask for much, does she?"

The trio of stooges clanked their beers and drank. Craig marveled at their synchronized stupidity. He was as irritated as he was amused. They had not changed since high school. Alcohol had boosted their foolhardiness. The four of them together were probably incapable of finding their way out of a one-lane labyrinth.

Craig shot a look over at Susannah who was absorbed in conversation with the equally incompetent female triumvirate. He glanced at his watch: 9:37 p.m. *Dear Lord*. The night hadn't even begun. He had hoped to get out at a reasonable time so he could spend time with Athena.

"Hey! I'm talking to you," Jake shoved an iron finger into Craig's chest.

"What? What did you say?" Craig resisted the urge to massage the area.

"He asked you how you managed to score Suzy, you being a candyass." Charles shot a look over at the ladies and pointed at Susannah with his beer. "That's a whole lotta woman for you."

"Well, uh . . ." Craig gleamed and shrugged his shoulders. "I guess you can call it a little bit of luck and love. You guys should try it some time." He rocked gently on his heels like a schoolboy who has just scored his first date and laughed internally as he saw the expressions of the men, especially Jake's, go sour.

"You think you're funny, don't you?" Jake handed the beer to Hugh and drew closer. The smile evaporated.

I hope he doesn't start something. Not here. Not now. Craig's heart raced. The victory was short-lived. His body tensed for an incoming blow.

"Watch it, man." Hugh laughed. "I think he just wet his pants like in the locker room."

Craig's mind raced back to that one moment in the locker room during their senior year when Jake snuck up behind him as they were changing after gym class and landed one square in the ribs. The pain had caused him to urinate on himself. The others had roared as Craig doubled over with a stream running down the side of his legs. The memory made him shudder.

Craig felt a modest tug on his arm and flinched. Susannah wrapped her arm around his. "So what are you guys talking about?"

"Ribs." Jake smiled.

"Impossible. We're vegetarians. No meat in our house."

Craig looked over and smiled at her cleverness.

"May as well satisfy your needs with a cucumber, baby," Jake laughed. "There's not enough meat here to cover a chicken bone." He placed a thorny hand on Craig's shoulder and squeezed. The pain shot through his shoulder. He shrugged it off amid laughter.

Sally barged into the scene like a welcomed parasite, yanking Susannah away with the other women. Susannah stole a nervous glance over her shoulder at Craig who gave her thumbs-up. Jake made no attempt to avoid staring at Susannah's ass as it disappeared into the crowd. He loosened his tie.

"Mighty fine lady you got there, Helmethead. Yes siree. Great fucking ass." He reached for Craig's shoulder, but Craig slapped his hand away.

"Her name is Susannah," Craig stated bluntly. "And she's no great *fucking* piece of ass. She's my wife. Don't be an asshole all your life, Jake. Grow the fuck up." His body shook slightly from a combination of fear and anger. *If only I was bigger.*

"To you, she's Susannah." Jake shrugged. "To me, well, she's a great piece of ass. What can I say?" His henchmen laughed.

Craig cursed himself for not talking Susannah out of coming here.

"Let's go." Hugh tugged at Jake's shoulder. "This is bullshit."

"Fuck you both." Craig swore under his breath and was amazed that the words had come out of his mouth. They certainly felt good coming out; he just hoped they wouldn't be the epitaph on his tombstone. He desired something honorable on that marble slab, something like "Here Lies a Good Man, a Loving Husband, and a Devoted Father," but definitely not "Fuck You Both."

"Well, well." Hugh stopped. "Looks like our little candyass has finally grown a pair." He handed his drink to Jake and pressed a finger to Craig's chest in the same area as Jake had. It felt as if he was being poked with a tire iron. "How's about I take those marble nuts of yours, along with your words, and shove them down your throat?" He searched Craig's eyes.

Hugh's breath reeked of beer, liquor, and cigarette. Craig thought about tossing a match into his mouth and watch him blow up into a million pieces. Instead, he backed off. "Just leave me alone. I don't want any trouble, please." He stared at Hugh and sighed. "Let's just forget the whole thing." *Suzy, where are you? Let's leave this cursed place.*

The four horsemen left amid a cacophony of laughter, high fives, and backslaps. Craig walked around searching for a friendly face, but none of his friends were there. Had he been the only one gullible enough to have fallen into this trap? He found Susannah in a circle of women absorbed in laughter. Several people passed by him and smiled faintly. He made his way toward the circle hoping that Susannah would agree to leave this miserable place, but as he approached the group, more laughter broke out. Susannah was doubled over grabbing her stomach. He took a detour to the bar.

10:21 p.m.

The evening became more pleasant and tolerable with every drink. He kept to himself the entire night, contemplating the DJ. Billy Joel's "Glass Houses" CD caught his eye, and when he reached for it, the DJ told him to "Fuck off."

At about eleven o'clock, the music was placed on hold for a couple of speeches. Mr. Coles, the retired principal and a facsimile of Elmer Fudd, made his way to the microphone with the help of a cane and began waving at the crowd as if he had received an Oscar. He thanked everybody in attendance, gave a brief history of Fairfield High and how the rich tradition has been carried on by current students, faculty, and staff, and proceeded to ask Coach Sykes onto the stage. *Sorry, kid, you're just not cut out for football or baseball. Perhaps sports isn't your thing. Why don't you try other things like the science and chess clubs.* The words had been imprinted in Craig's mind. He cursed Coach Sykes back then, and he cursed him now. *Asshole.* Coach Sykes's dedication to the school went no further than the football team. Life for him was a football analogy. According to him, if you couldn't launch a football fifty yards down the field, you were merely occupying valuable turf space on this earth. He blabbered on about the history of Fairfield High's athletic achievements for what seemed an eternity. Craig watched from the bleachers as a group of ex-jocks, now professional assholes, gathered in front of the podium for their deification. Jake and his henchmen pumped their fists into the air and made loud "whooping" sounds every time Coach Sykes recalled an event. After having hosed down the floor of the gymnasium with elephantine levels of testosterone, Sykes dismissed the crowd and ordered everybody to have a good time at the blow of his whistle. Elton John's "Crocodile Rock" poured from the speakers.

I remember when rock was young, me and Suzy had so much fun . . .

"Having a good time?" Susannah appeared and handed Craig a drink.

"Of course," he lied. "Wouldn't miss it for the world."

"Liar." She adjusted her dress and sat down next to him on the bleachers. "Is everything okay?" She caressed the back of his neck. "Why aren't you out there talking to the guys?"

"I'm having a great time. Really."

"For a minute there, I thought Jake was going to pull off one of his asshole acts." She took a sip from the plastic cup. "What did you guys talk about?"

We talked about what a great ass you have. Actually, a great fucking piece of ass. "Oh, not much. Mostly careers." *Why can't we just go home? I have to attend to our daughter.*

"Want to dance?" She finished her drink and gave him a pat on the knee.

"Sure. Why not?" Craig finished his drink and threw the cup underneath the bleachers. "Oops." They made their way to center court. Years of absence from the dance floor manifested themselves in their movements, especially his. Every time Susannah swung to the left, he swung to the right. When she moved to the right, he moved to the left. He headbutted and stepped on her shoes a couple of times. Susannah laughed and embraced him, kissing him softly, whispering "I love you" in his ear. She was enjoying herself, and he had just the right amount of alcohol in him not to give a damn whether he looked like a fool or not.

After the third song, he loosened up and stated that attending the reunion had actually been a marvelous idea. With every song, years seem to fall off the calendar until the euphoria placed them back in high school. They had not met until the second half of their junior year. His mind went back to the moment they first met at the library when he was spying on her from behind the shelves . . .

January 27, 1988, 11:36 a.m.

He had been staring at her for almost half an hour through shelves, taking in her coal-black hair, which she brushed aside nonchalantly, causing his heart to race faster. Almond skin, shapely thighs and legs, and a face capable of launching a million ships. She turned the pages of a textbook gracefully while arching her back. He traced every curvature of her body through the bright orange tank top and thigh-high jean skirt. When other students walked by, he would flip a couple of pages of the book in his hand and pretend to read. As soon as everybody cleared, he resumed his voyeurism. She ran her hand through her hair and held it there while thumping the pencil on the table. She seemed to be struggling with the reading, and several times, he was on the verge of uprooting himself from the spot to help her but was stalled by intermittent appearances from guys who sat down to chat. Craig's shoulders would sag until she kindly told them that she had to study. The guys left. This was his chance. He dragged his quivering body over and sat two chairs from her. Their eyes met for a fraction of a second, sending an arctic frigidity through his body. The chair screeched as he pulled it out gently. He shot her an apologetic smile. When he was finally seated, he did everything to avoid her stare. After several minutes of pregnant silence, Craig turned to her.

"I'm—"

"Hey, Suzy Q." A girl perched herself on the table: it was Sally Forrester. The golden-brown highlights in her long, bouncy golden hair, and a deeply tanned skin screamed countless hours and constant visits to hair and tanning salons. A shiny, light metallic-blue eye shadow, bloodred lipstick, and eyelashes the length of rakes gave her a look more apt for a Hollywood Boulevard hooker than a high school student. "You going to the party after the game tomorrow night?"

Susannah used the pencil as a bookmark, closed it, and leaned back. "Oh, I don't know. I got some more studying to do. The exam is on Monday." She paused. "Who's going?"

"Duh! Like everybody." Sally leaned closer. "Jake and the guys are going to be there," she giggled.

"Sorry. I don't think so. I really have to study," Susannah responded.

Craig's heart cheered her on.

"Jake was asking about you."

"Not interested." Susannah shook her head.

"Come on, he's gorgeous." Sally pressed on. "*And* he's the captain of the football team. Like what's not to like?"

"I don't care if he's Captain America, I'm just not interested." Susannah opened her textbook. "I really want to pass this test."

"I don't see what the big deal is." Sally stood up. "You can always take it next year." She leaned over. "And you can always ask Mr. Trent for a little *extra* help. He grades the exams, you know." She nudged Susannah. "He helped Barbara."

Sally smiled as her eyebrows danced up and down.

"Oh, please, Sally." Susannah held up a hand. "You're disturbed, and you're both going to get caught."

"Maybe." Sally grinned. "Maybe not. But it is kinda erotic, totally, like living out a fantasy."

"A sick one at that." Susannah returned to the book. "Listen, I don't want to wait until next year," she challenged. "Besides, at least I'll know what to expect if I don't pass."

You go, girl, Craig's mind yelled.

"Suit yourself." Sally shrugged her shoulders. "Your loss. But if you change your mind, call me. Kisses." She left.

Susannah sighed and stared at the pages.

Craig swallowed hard and took a deep breath. He licked his lips. *This is it!* He dug into his bookbag, took out the same textbook, and placed it so that Susannah could read the title on the spine. He noticed Susannah staring at the book and took out his notebook and a calculator. Within seconds, he was busy scribbling, punching keys, and scribbling some more. This went on for about two minutes. All the while, Susannah's occasional glances had turned into a flat-out stare, which served as a catalyst for Craig.

"Lucky you," she said.

"Excuse me?" Craig's continued to write, pretending not to have heard. The inside of his mouth became a desert.

"I said"—she sat up straight and pointed at the textbook—"you must be lucky to know all that stuff."

Craig found himself staring at the Amazonian he was always admiring from behind books, pillars, trees, and the back of the classroom. Her lips revealed a hidden sexuality, her eyes a hypnotic oceanic blue capable of complete seduction with just one stare, and sable hair that flared out in gentle, soothing waves.

"Uh . . . oh . . . uh . . . yeah." He cleared his throat and blinked. She was still smiling. He looked at equations and numbers as they danced on the pages before him and back to her. "Yes, it is," he replied while straightening up. This time, he returned the smile. "It's really not that difficult. I . . . I could show you, if . . . if you want."

"Aren't we in the same class?" She cocked her head. "You sit all the way in the back by the projector, right?"

"Yeah, that's me."

"Greg."

"Craig."

"Right." She shook her head. "Well . . . uh . . . sure . . . , if you don't mind."

He began to explain.

Susannah cut him short. "It would be better if you came closer, don't you think?" She raised her eyebrows.

He slid his books over and floated toward her, bumping her knee and offering a hundred apologies. With every second that passed, barriers were broken, equations were explained, and a fondness for one another was germinated. They shared several anecdotes that resulted in laughter. During one story, she was so caught up in her laughter that she inadvertently, or purposely, placed her hand on top of his. Craig experienced some wooziness and had to clamp his jaws shut to keep his heart from leaping out. They had skipped lunch, exchanged numbers, and agreed to meet over the next two days to study for the SATs. Although it was nothing more than studying on Friday afternoons and Saturday mornings, to Craig they may as well have been dates. And it was on a Saturday that he suggested they get a bite to eat after three hours of studying. Life could not have scripted a better weekend for Craig, until the results of the exams came in, that is. She had scored a 1,350 while he scored a 1,570.

"Oh, my god . . . I passed!" She hugged him and cemented an exaggerated kiss on his cheek. "Thank you, thank you, thank you. I couldn't have done it without you."

"Oh, it was nothing." Craig restrained himself from hugging her back and proclaiming eternal love. "You knew the equations all along. All I did was help."

"Let's celebrate." She clasped her hands.

"Celebrate?"

"Yeah. Dinner and a movie. My treat. A little something to show my appreciation."

That first friendly date eventually turned into something more. A smorgasbord of rumors surfaced once the word was out. "Girl, like what do you see in him? You could get any boy you want. Instead of a hero, you got a zero," Sally remarked with a look as if she had bitten into a rotten egg.

"It's not like that at all. He's different," Susannah replied.

"No shit."

"Listen. He makes me laugh and is fun to be around. He treats me nice and is respectful, not trying to get into my pants like everybody else," she challenged.

"Maybe he's like gay, totally." Sally shrugged.

"I don't think so. Anyway, I like him. And if you're my friend, you should be happy for me, not insult me. I mean, I don't say anything about Ray, and you know for a fact that he's a bona fide asshole."

"Yeah, but he's hot and awesome." Sally curled her lips. "Totally."

From there on, conversations about her going out with Craig died down. Although they tolerated his presence, he would never be accepted into their inner sanctum.

Their relationship grew stronger while attending the same college, was eventually solidified in marriage, and guided them to this reunion. Even here, even now, Craig's love for his wife continued to grow.

10:59 p.m.

"I'm glad you came," Jake shouted over the music.

"Thank you," Craig replied as the memory evaporated. *Aw shit. What now?*

"Not you, asshole." Jake chuckled. He leaned back and looked at Susannah. "Suzy Q."

Susannah smiled defensively and stood next to Craig; he shared her caution.

"How's about one dance, sweetheart." Jake pushed his way between the couple with his back to Craig.

Susannah was caught off guard. One arm snaked around her waist while the other squeezed her ass. His breath reeked of alcohol. She looked desperately over his shoulder at Craig while trying to break free. "Jake! Stop it!" She wrestled with the vice grip. He tightened his hold and began to grind his hips.

Was it the alcohol? Fear? Courage? Or just plain stupidity? Perhaps all, perhaps just a man defending his wife. Craig grabbed onto one of Jake's arms; it felt like pulling open a huge wooden cathedral door.

"You son-of-a-bitch! Let go of my wife!" The anger within escalated to new heights but did nothing in the way of enhancing his strength. It did serve, however, to amuse Jake, and he responded by pressing his lips to Susannah's. She squirmed as his liquor-soaked tongue searched for hers. Craig grabbed him by the collar, and for a second, the three of them were dancing.

Jake finally released his strong hold on Susannah. The dancing stopped. A growing circle of spectators surrounded the trio. Sally ran over to Susannah, who was on the verge of tears. Susannah shrugged her off. The men stood face-to-face. Sally laughed. Someone must have informed the DJ of what was happening because the music came to an abrupt halt. The crowd stirred.

"What's the matter, asshole? Can't let your wife have a good time with a *real* man?" Jake gave Craig a stiff shove that sent him reeling backward with his arms flailing, causing the crowd to respond with a mixture of gasps and laughter, among them Jake's cronies.

"Somebody do something!" Somebody shouted.

"Craig!" Susannah yelled. She tried to break free from Sally who held her back with an amused smile.

"Fuck you, Jake!" Craig shared the desperation in his wife's eyes. He heard some of the staff trying to make their way through the crowd, but the wall of people would not yield. Some of the guys from the football team joined hands to form a chain. There would be no help.

"Fuck me?" Jake shoved Craig even more violently. "Yeah, you'd like that, wouldn't you?"

Susannah was being restrained by her "friends." Craig surmised that this had all been planned. The high school reunion was nothing but a devious plot to get back at him for having the nerve to step into "their" world and steal one of "their" maidens, a plot twenty years in the making. Indeed the plate was cold, and it would be served tonight. *If only I had the Ring of Gyges.* He thrust a trembling finger at Jake. "Y-you keep your s-stinking hands off of my wife." He let out a yelp as Jake grabbed his finger and bent it backwards, bringing him to his knees. Every time Craig reached for his hands, Jake twisted harder causing more pain. The crowd grew restless; there was more laughter.

"Let him go!" Susannah yelled. She elbowed Sally in the chest, pushed her back, and ran to Craig. She stood by her husband's side and screamed at Jake. "Let him go!" Her hands were balled into fists as she scanned the crowd for help.

"Tell you what, buddy." Jake laughed. "You let me show your wife a good time, and I promise you'll be out of the hospital in only one week."

The veins in Craig's temples pulsed as he beheld the tears in Susannah's eyes. Ignoring the pain, he sat up just enough to get a clean shot at Jake's groin. He pulled his arm back, made a fist, closed his eyes, and launched his arm forward with all of his might. Jake released his grip, grabbed his crotch, and doubled over. A series of "Oohs" and "Ahhs" burst from the crowd. Craig got up flexing his fingers and grabbed Susannah by the arm. "Let's go!"

They pushed through the crowd, but Hugh and some other guys kept shoving them back. Somebody screamed and another yelled "Watch out!" but it was too late. Jake was upon them. He grabbed Craig's jacket and rammed him into one of the banquet tables. Craig's face crashed with the punch bowl. As he attempted to straighten up, he grabbed onto the tablecloth and slipped, taking several trays with him to the ground. Bread rolls and macaroni salad went flying, landing on his chest. The cocktail sauce splattered on Craig's face and concealed the blood flowing from the gash on the side of his forehead. Susannah grabbed onto one of Jake's arms to no avail. She looked like a ten-year-old trying to hold back a mastiff. Jake shoved her to the ground as he approached Craig. The fury in his eyes spelled disaster for Craig, who scrambled on the floor like an insect and grabbed a hold of a serving tray. As Jake cocked his arm back for what would have been countless hours of reconstructive facial surgery and cost thousands of dollars, Craig swung the tray and caught him square on the nose. *Thud!* The blood oozed through Jake's hands as he grabbed his nose.

"Motherfucker!" Jake yelled.

Craig got up to run but slipped on the mixture of macaroni salad and fruit punch, giving Jake that extra second he needed. Meat hooks sunk into Craig's shoulders and spun him around like a top. The wetness of the floor prevented him from regaining his balance. He clawed frantically at Jake's shirt who assumed a boxer's stance, chambering his right arm like a piston.

"Craig!" Susannah screamed at the top of her lungs.

Craig looked over Jake's massive fist and saw Susannah on the floor reaching helplessly for him. Jake curled his lips into a malevolent grin. As the wrecking ball descended, he locked onto Jake's eyes. "Fuck you to hell," he grunted. The impact blackened out the entire scenario except for the constellation of black and white speckles that swum around in his eyes.

11:17 p.m.

"Craig? Honey? Are you okay?" Susannah cradled her husband in her lap like a comical relief of Michelangelo's *Pieta*. A cocktail-stained tablecloth lay at her feet as she cleaned his face.

After the coup de grâce, the human chain gave way to teachers that had been wrestling to get through. Mr. Coles jostled his way through, bumping people with his cane in the process. "Shoo, shoo. Make way, make way. Give him room. Stand back. Give him room." He adjusted his glasses and looked at Susannah. "Is he okay?"

Craig groaned.

"Are you okay, young man?"

Craig opened his eyes slowly to a hazy world. The three images became two. He squinted hard and then they became one: it was Susannah.

"Thank God you're all right." She kissed him on the forehead.

"Where are we?" He looked at the crowd and sat up.

"Let's go home." Susannah rubbed his back. She got to her feet and helped him up. "Let's get out of here," she said while brushing off shrimp and lettuce from his jacket. Her smile quickly turned into tears. "I'm so sorry." She buried her face in her hands.

"It's okay." Craig pulled Susannah toward him and began to stroke her hair. "I'm okay." He kissed the top of her head. "Let's just go home. I don't like the shrimp cocktail anyway."

The crowd had begun to disperse. Some stared and pointed fingers at him while others sniggered.

"Did you see that?"

"Wow! Can't believe he's still standing."

"Who started it?"

"He was out cold."

"How embarrassing."

An intense loathing surfaced within Craig at the last comment. The entire evening seemed to have been scripted with him as the main event. A couple who seemed genuinely worried about the laceration on his forehead and Susannah's crying were quickly dismissed with a resounding "No!" followed by a "Get away from us! We don't need any help." *And where were you, any of you, all of you, while I was getting pounded and humiliated?* Anger turned to rage. He began to guide Susannah through the horde when he felt someone grab him by the arm.

"Excuse me." Mr. Coles produced a handkerchief and offered it to Craig. "Are you going to be all right, young man? Is there anything I can do, Susannah? I'm terribly sorry for this most unfortunate incident."

Craig shook his head. *Geez, he doesn't even remember my name.*

"No, thank you, Mr. Coles. We just want to go home." She tugged at Craig's arm. "Come on."

The speakers came alive once again as a recognizable tune reached Craig's ears, freezing him in his tracks.

"Rising up, back on my feet, did my time, took my chances . . .

Went the distance now I'm back on my feet,

Just a man and his will to survive."

He looked in the general direction of the DJ as the words reverberated in his ears.

"It's the eye of the tiger, the thrill of the fight . . ."

Coincidence? Or had the DJ purposely chosen this song?

"Craig, come on." Susannah tugged on his arm. "Please, let's just go."

As they neared the exit, he caught sight of Ted, Charlie, Hugh, Sally, and the other two women. Ted slapped Hugh on the shoulder and thumbed in their direction. Hugh stepped aside, and there was Jake sitting down, holding a bloody napkin to his nose. Sally made as if to approach Susannah, but the scorn she received from Susannah warned her to stand down. She pursed her lips and shrugged her shoulders: the other two women laughed.

"Just keep walking." Susannah tightened her grip.

"Hey!"

Craig stopped and turned as Jake approached. *Oh boy, here we go again.* This time, he felt more annoyed than afraid. Perhaps the blow to his head had dulled his senses. Jake removed the bloody napkin revealing tissue stuffed into each of his nostrils. Craig laughed inwardly.

"You won't be so lucky next time, faggot," Jake said loudly.

"There won't be a next time, asshole," Susannah challenged as she pulled on Craig even harder. "Come."

"Maybe next time, I'll fight your wife. She seems to have more balls than you," Jake roared. The other three miscreants joined in on the laughter. And after a second or two, so did Sally and the two women.

As they exited the school, flashing blue-and-red lights bounced off them. Coach Sykes was standing on the steps and pointed at the couple. A police officer approached Craig and asked if he had been one of the participants in the fight.

"Lucky guess," he responded. "Tell me, Officer, how does one actually *participate* in a fight? And a fight, by my definition, is between two people. What happened here is more like an assault." For the next ten minutes, Craig recounted his embarrassing episode: from Jake's commentaries about Susannah's ass to momentarily visiting the spirit world after Jake's fist collided with his head. The officer stared at the cut on his forehead and the red-stained shirt. He pointed at it with his pen.

"Cocktail sauce," he replied while staring at his shirt.

The officer nodded and asked if he would like to come down to the station and file a formal report and perhaps press charges.

"I just want to forget the entire thing ever happened." He rubbed Susannah's shoulder. "Are we done? Can we leave?"

"You might want to have that cut looked at, sir," the officer stated.

"Sure, no problem," Craig responded without even looking back.

They drove home in silence. Susannah demanded to drive, but Craig dismissed her. "I'm okay, honestly. Please, let me drive."

She sat with her arms crossed and kept a watchful eye on him as he negotiated every curve. "Are you okay? Does it hurt? You want to pull over and let me drive? Are you getting dizzy? Would you like me to take you to the hospital?"

"Yes, no, no, no, and no," he responded.

"Fine," she responded, only to begin rephrasing the questions: "How do you feel? Is it painful? Can I drive the rest of the way while you rest? Is your vision okay? I think you should have that looked at, don't you think?"

They finally arrived at the house, and not a moment too soon, he threw up on Susannah's lilies as soon as he got out the car.

"I told you you should've let me drive." She helped him to the door. "Are you sure you don't want to go to the hospital?"

"Positive." He smiled and pushed open the door. He threw his jacket on the sofa; it slipped and fell to the floor. Susannah picked it up, folded it, and placed it on the kitchen counter. Craig unbuttoned his shirt on the way to the bathroom. He turned on the faucet and splashed cold water on his face several times, wincing as it came into contact with the cut on his forehead. Bracing himself on the sink, he stared into the mirror. A thin line of blood and water ran down the side of his face and detoured onto his chin creating a thin jagged red line just to the left of his lip that made his face resemble a jigsaw puzzle. Droplets of blood accumulated on the bottom of his chin, grew, then released their grip and fell to the sink. A small crimson amoeba-shaped blotch doubled in size against the white porcelain. The face in the mirror stared back in shame.

"Some hero," he muttered and sighed. He grabbed a towel and walked out. The bump on his forehead had grown considerably larger. Drilling a hole on the top of his head to relieve pressure seemed like a pretty good idea right about now.

AL BRUNO

"Careful. Don't touch it." Susannah walked over with the first aid kit and a beer. "Here. Drink this while I take care of that nasty cut."

Craig sat down heavily and kicked off his shoes. He closed his eyes and leaned his head back, wondering if the entire night had indeed taken place. It all seemed surreal. Were it not for the laceration compliments of Jake, he could have easily forgotten the entire ordeal. Arguing his decision on not wanting to go would only serve to drive the guilt deeper into his wife's heart. During the drive home, she had offered a hundred apologies through tears, claiming that it was all her fault and had they not gone, none of this would have happened. This was their first and last reunion.

"It's not your fault. Ouch!"

"Sorry." She dabbed at the cut with cotton balls saturated in hydrogen peroxide. "I think it would be better if you rest your head on my lap." She made her way around the sofa and sat down. "Here," she patted her thighs; Craig lay down.

"I'm just furious at the whole thing, especially Sally. What a bitch she turned out to be." She grabbed a new set of cotton balls. "If anyone deserved to get hit, it was her."

"Don't sweat it." He opened his eyes. "People like her and Jake always get what they deserve." He paused. "Sooner or late, they get theirs."

"Yeah, well, I'd like to be the one giving it to them." Susannah capped the bottle of peroxide and reached for the iodine.

"Ow, ow! Not so hard."

"I don't want it to get infected."

"By the way, what exactly happened?" He relaxed his body and shut his eyes.

"You were out for a minute or so." Susannah stroked his hair. "And you have a nasty bruise."

Craig probed the bump on his forehead.

"Careful." She pushed his hand away.

"Sorry to have ruined your evening."

"I'm sorry too." She caressed his hair and leaned over.

"You must think I'm some kind of jerk."

"Not at all." She lifted her head. "You're a wonderful man, and I'm the luckiest woman in the world."

"So am I forgiven?"

"Yes." She kissed his cheek. "I'm very proud of you, my knight in shining armor."

"And cocktail sauce," he added.

"I love you," she added while caressing his chest.

Susannah suggested they light the fireplace and savor what remained of the evening. Craig worked on preparing the fire while she went in search of something to drink, returning with two glasses and a bottle of red wine. Once the fire got going, he crawled on all fours to the sofa and pulled himself up. She handed him a glass.

"And what is it exactly that we're toasting to?" he asked.

She stared at the glass.

"Hey, you okay?" He leaned forward.

"To us." She forced a smile accompanied by two lines of tears. "We have each other." She clanked his glass and drank heartily.

Craig finished his wine and took her face in his hands as he wiped away the tears with his thumbs.

"It's okay," she cried. "I'm okay."

Conversation was held to a minimum. After the first bottle, no more words were spoken. Craig came back with a second bottle. Susannah's eyes were beginning to haze, but she insisted on having *one more glass*. She laid her head on his lap; he stroked her hair. They drank in silence, staring deep into the flaming tongues of the fire. Wood crackled, split, and was devoured by the fiery entity, sending sparks and small pieces of ember airborne that quickly disintegrated into the air. Two and a half bottles later, Susannah surrendered to a combination of exhaustion and wine. Craig grabbed what remained of the third bottle and chugged; some of it escaped his mouth and ran down his chin. He wiped it with the back of his hand, leaned his head back, closed his eyes, and took a deep breath. The crackling sound and warmth of the fire along with the cool, tranquil breeze coming in through the window lulled him into a cavernous slumber.

He ran from locker to locker desperately seeking refuge, pulling against the bigger lockers, hoping to open one and jump inside. The further he went down the line, the more lockers appeared. He scanned as far down as he could see; there was no end to the lockers. Only row after row after row. He staggered to a halt and placed his hands on his knees gulping for air.

"Craigee . . . Craigee . . . Craigee . . . Hey, Helmethead, we're coming for you." The echoes were accompanied by a chorus of laughter.

Craig whirled his head left and right and resumed running. This time, the configuration of the locker rooms changed—there were openings! With renewed vigor, Craig zigzagged through the metallic labyrinth. Every

AL BRUNO

corner promised an exit but produced only a myriad of more turns. He stopped at an intersection.

"Hey, Helmethead, how's Suzy? That's a mighty fine piece of ass you got there. Mind if me and the boys spend some time with her?" Jake's metallic laughter reverberated through the maze.

Craig clasped his head and grimaced.

"I'll show her what a real man is. You wouldn't mind, would you, Craigee? After all, we're all high school buddies, aren't we, Helmethead?"

"Fuck you, Jake!" Craig balled his fists and began swinging at the air. "Go to hell. Stay away from us!"

"Athena . . . Suzy doesn't know about her, does she?" Jake's laughter catapulted Craig's anger to new heights.

Craig dropped panting to one knee, pressing a trembling hand to his mouth.

"Why, you ain't even man enough to give her a real child."

"Son-of-a-bitch! Shut up! You leave my little girl out of this." He sprang to his feet and yelled in all directions. "I'll kill you, Jake. You come near my baby, and I'll kill you!"

"Ha ha ha. Baby? Little girl? It's an abomination from hell, a monster. You created it. You're responsible. You did it, you did it, you did it . . ."

June 30, 2009, 1:17 a.m.

Craig twitched violently, sending the empty bottle of wine across the rug, watching as it came to rest at the base of the fireplace. Dying flames danced across the reflection on the glassy surface making it appear as if the bottle itself was on fire.

Susannah stirred then resumed her snoring.

He squeezed his eyes and ran a hand across his face. The fire slowly vanished as it gave way to the grim darkness of the woods that crept into the house like a shrouded villain. Curtains danced tenderly amid the gentle fingers of the air, capturing the illumination of the moon on their fabric, furnishing them with an eerie, foreboding glow, yet hypnotically inviting the soul into the heart of the woods.

Craig laid Susannah's hand gently on the couch and kissed her on the forehead before draping her with a quilt. He picked up the bottle of wine. One of the logs split and fell, causing the other logs to shift, sending another platoon of tiny embers airborne. He covered his face and leaned back, brushing them off of his arms. Susannah was fast asleep. In the kitchen, he took out a tray of ice cubes and banged it against the sink—some fell to the floor—stuffed a sandwich bag with ice and pressed it against his forehead. At first it stung a little, but after a minute or two, the cold felt good against his skin. Holding the bag of ice firmly against his forehead, he walked over to the refrigerator and grabbed three beers that were still attached to the plastic ring. While the ice soothed the pain in his head, the beer nullified the pain in his heart.

He sat on the kitchen stool and downed two beers before deciding to take a walk and see his daughter. With everything that had happened tonight, he had totally forgotten to bring Athena her food. He was abashed for having forgotten to take care of his daughter at the usual time.

She must be waiting for me. Probably worried.

The thought infuriated him even more. He would have preferred to spend the evening with his daughter than attend that stupid reunion. Jake's escapades had rendered the evening a catastrophe, and now, it had almost made him forget the most important thing in his life. He microwaved a couple of pieces of fried chicken and grabbed a couple of apples. He didn't think she liked apples until one day he was biting into one, and she snatched it out of his mouth, smelled it, and turned it over in her hands before biting into it. At first, she chewed slowly, and then the apple was gone in two powerful bites. Ever since then, he brought a couple of apples every other day.

Craig got dressed, grabbed the food and a couple more beers, and made his way to the door. He stared at Susannah and took a deep breath.

"I'm gonna see Athena, honey. I'll tell her Mommy sends her love." He closed the door gently.

In the garage, he kept a medium-sized refrigerator with a secret stash of food. There he kept hot dogs, cold cuts, boxes of chicken, and a variety of frozen food entrees. Since he was currently restoring his '72 Ford Mustang, he often spent late afternoons and weekends in the garage. Ever since he had left a trail of greasy footprints and oily thumbprints on the plates, glass, and container of orange juice, Susannah had forbidden him to enter the house after he had been in the garage. It was therefore decided that he keep his own little fridge and microwave in the garage. The arrangement worked out quite well since she rarely came into the garage much less inspect the fridge. She went as far as the entrance of the garage and addressed him, not wanting to get grease on her shoes as well. And when he finished working on the car, the boots *had* to come off *before* he left the garage to avoid staining the thousands of dollars' worth of work they had spent on the Etruscan paving stones that covered the driveway and walkways to the house.

He took out the bread, cold cuts, and cheese, made a couple of sandwiches, and grabbed a jug of ice-cold water because she hadn't had fresh water for a couple of days.

Occasionally, Craig made his way through the woods with the aid of a flashlight. But after thousands of trips to and from the tree house, the flashlight had become more of an emergency tool than a necessity. The shapes of trees and foliage and their respective location with regards to the path leading to the tree house was all the map he needed. So adept had he become that he could tell whether he was headed in the right direction just by looking at the dark silhouettes of the branches overhead. Within many of them, he had created a host of mental images that served as reference points.

The cool timid breeze of the forest encircled his body, providing a soft blanket of ominous security and purity endemic to the forest. The aroma of pine combs and musky grass overran his senses. An owl greeted him in its own language. Cicadas provided the chorus as the sound of the wind pushing against the branches completed the melodious tunes of the forest.

After having navigated over twenty minutes through the arboreal labyrinth, Craig came upon the downed tree that lay against another tree to create an isosceles triangle, which signified the path to the tree house. Once past this natural geometric architecture, it was but another hundred feet or so. He jumped over a three-foot stream that ran parallel to the tree house. This was Athena's source of water as well as bathing site. During the warm months, he brought soap, towels, and a bottle of Susannah's perfume and bathe his daughter. As she got older, she would sometimes wrestle him into the stream; he would dump his wet clothes at the foot of the washing machine and use the excuse that the sprinkler had suddenly turned on during the night as he was checking something in the garage. She never questioned his loyalty, much less his wet clothes.

Craig approached the tree house and called out to his daughter.

"Athena, honey, Daddy's here."

A shadow detached itself from the dark silhouette of the tree, a pair of yellow orbs accompanied the specter as it made its way toward Craig. At first, she grunted and walked cautiously sniffing the air, then broke into a slight trot like a gorilla charging an intruder, covering the distance between her and Craig with alarming speed.

"Come to Daddy, baby." Craig smiled and knelt as the creature advanced. He held out his arms.

Athena bumped into Craig and came to a sudden halt sending him backward onto the damp grass. Before he could sit up, a coarse tongue landed on his cheek repeatedly like an angry painter trying to cover up a stain on a wall. Craig grasped and stroked the creature's head as he struggled to get her off of him.

"My goodness, Athena. I gotta put you on a diet." He got up, dusted himself, and grabbed the bag of goodies. "Where's my beer?"

Craig and his daughter walked hand-in-hand to a log just past the tree house, where he sat to finish his beer.

"Sorry, I'm late. Daddy ran into some trouble tonight." He sighed. "More like Jake's fist, but no harm done. Daddy's here." He dug his hand in the bag and took out the sandwiches and chicken. "You hungry?"

Athena ignored her food, pressed her nose against his hands, inhaling scents until finally reaching the laceration on his forehead.

"Hey! Careful."

Powerful, calloused fingers with talonlike fingernails gingerly probed the area. Craig winced.

"That's just a little bump. Nothing to worry about. Daddy's okay." He caressed her wrinkled cheeks. She licked the wound and placed a hand on his chest, sniffing him and inhaling deeply. Athena stroked his hair and made a low-pitched groan.

"Athena, baby, I'm okay." Tears sprang from his eyes. "Really. I'm fine. Just a little bruise."

For the next hour, father and daughter shared the silence of the woods and the coolness of the night. Craig caressed the furry head on his lap. Athena purred. She would often jerk her head in the direction of a noise audible only to her. Craig stared into the darkness in absence of fear: Athena was with him. Tonight, however, she had barely touched her food. Her entire demeanor had changed after discovering the wounds on his face. Craig gave her an anecdotal of the tragic play that had unfolded tonight and its main antagonist—Jake. Athena would cock her head and lick his wound every so often, finishing with a hug that threatened to shatter his rib cage.

Craig yawned and nearly fell backwards. His eyelids fluttered as exhaustion crept into his body. He left the food and water and kissed Athena on top of her head.

"Gotta go, sweetheart. Mommy's all alone." She stared as he walked away. He blew his daughter a kiss before crossing the stream. All he wanted was to sleep for about a week and forget the entire evening. A couple of

AL BRUNO

paces into the woods, he turned around. Athena's eyes shone in the distance like menacing candles, and for the first time ever, he shuddered in the presence of his daughter. He dismissed the fear and staggered through the woods, stopping occasionally to catch his breath and reorient himself.

He reached the house and eased the door shut; Susannah's snoring resembled a broken muffler. After washing his face, Craig went over to the window and looked into the blackness of the woods. There was something different tonight, something sinister. Athena's stare had made him uneasy, and he had found himself double-timing it back home. He closed the window and lay at the foot of the sofa with a beer. After two sips, he collapsed into a deep slumber.

9:12 a.m.

Susannah opened her eyes to a world draped in fog. She squeezed them hard and yawned. The blanket fell onto Craig's face as she sat up. She brushed it aside and blinked several times until everything cleared up.

"Uh," she pressed her thumbs against her temples in small circles before sliding over on the sofa and standing on two shaky legs. She kicked Craig's foot, but he just turned to his side and curled up in a fetal position. As she made her way around, her right foot collided with the sofa. She cursed and hopped three times on one leg before planting it and hobbling over to the kitchen. She placed three scoops of coffee into the plastic cup, slid it into the coffee machine, pressed the On button, then made her way to the bathroom, turned on the shower, stripped, and stepped underneath the cascade. Goosebumps emerged on her arms and her teeth clattered before the hot water appeared. The events projected themselves as she bathed. There were faint bloodstains on her forearms from Craig's wound. She scrubbed vigorously with the soap over the area until it was red, and although the stain disappeared, what had taken place last night would not. Today was a new day, and with it the beginning of a healing process for both Craig's wounds and the humiliation. Her tears mixed in with the water as she remembered Craig discreetly expressing his lack of interest in wanting to attend the reunion; she should have picked up on the signs. Although he had not blamed her for what went down, she sensed an accusatory finger and blamed herself for pushing him into going. She sat down in the bathtub and wept.

Indeed, it's always a paltry, feeble, tiny mind that takes pleasure in revenge.

You can deduce it without further evidence than this, that no one delights more in vengeance than a woman.

—Juvenal (65?-128?)

August 4, 2009, 3:16 p.m.

CRAIG HAD LEFT work two hours early after an extremely productive day. An overly effervescent attitude had made his colleagues wonder whether the alleged "accident in the garage while replacing the coil springs on a shock absorber" had thrown his brain out of whack. The closing of a seven-million-dollar deal with a construction company had made his day, not to mention the nice commissions check for having sealed the deal. He could finally afford to get his Mustang reupholstered and buy a new differential, comparing this moment to the time he ripped the green-and-red paper decorated with Santa Claus flying over a cozy snow-covered cottage with his reindeer. He immediately donned his coat and begged to go outside and collect bugs, but his mother smiled and told him that bugs did not like the snow. *Oh.* He resorted to cockroach hunting with a flashlight. And when he came up empty, Mookie's tail hair provided to be just as exciting. After the first experiment, Mookie would scramble for cover and hide behind the couch with his tail between his legs at the sound of Craig's voice. When Craig discovered his hiding place, Mookie growled and refused to be taken captive, darting out from behind the sofa like a rock from a slingshot and straight into his mother's room.

Craig, what's wrong with Mookie?

Don't know, Mom. Maybe because it's bath time.

Craig chuckled as he turned the corner to his street, slowed down, and beeped the horn at Mr. Quincy, who was out playing remote-control cars with his grandson on the sidewalk. A sudden feeling of envy came over him but quickly evaporated as he pulled up to his house. A dark-blue sedan was parked in the driveway. They were not expecting any visitors, at least he wasn't. Susannah's friends? She did call in sick today. And that didn't look like any of her friends' car, at least not the one's he knew.

He pulled into the driveway and blocked the car; the ass end of his car on the sidewalk. He got out and peeked inside: a laptop on the center console, CB radio, a small, red beacon with a coiled extension, and several piles of paperwork and files in the backseat. Underneath the air-conditioning controls was a panel with about ten different buttons and toggle switches.

Craig placed his hands on his hips and looked around. *What the hell are the cops doing here?*

He made his way around the car and strode onto the porch; his heart began to race. Susannah! Had something happened to her? He grabbed the doorknob in one hand and keys in the other. It was unlocked. He stepped inside.

Susannah sat on the couch with a hand over her mouth. There were two men in dark suits and ties: one was sitting next to his wife with some papers in his hands while the other took in the pictures on the mantel. Her teary eyes widened, and she sprang off the couch as Craig stepped into the living room.

"Suzy? Are you okay?" Craig's heart stiffened.

"Oh Craig, thank God you're here." She reached for him with open arms and hugged him tightly.

"Everything's okay." He pried her hands off gently and placed her head between his hands and stroked her hair. "I'm here. Relax. Take a deep breath." She pressed her head into his shirt. Craig stared at the men. "Who the hell are you guys? What's going on here? What do you want with my wife?"

The taller of the two introduced himself as Detective Lyons, the one who had been looking at the pictures as Detective Fields.

"We're from Homicide," Lyons replied while pushing his jacket to the side, revealing a gold shield on his belt. Broad-shouldered, barrel-chested, with a slightly protruding belly, a square chin, and light olive-green eyes with bushy eyebrows and weathered cheekbones. Craig estimated him at about 6 feet 3 inches and about a solid 260 pounds. Most likely played high school and college football; perhaps a couple of years as pro before being cut or succumbing to an injury. And when the dreams faded away, he joined the force. His partner, Fields, was about Craig's build but, judging from his sinewy posture and sculptured shoulders, was obviously in serious shape. He had dark-brown eyes, superbly cropped hair—probably ex-military—with accents of gray, a chiseled face with a powerful jaw that made the muscles on his cheekbones dance as he chewed his gum, and a stare that could bring an innocent man to confess to crimes he had not committed.

"Homicide?" The word piqued his curiosity rather than strike concern.

Both men fixed their eyes on him as Lyons repeated the word with a bit more emphasis. They searched his face.

"Who's been murdered?" Craig detached himself from Susannah, approached Lyons, and turned to his wife. "Anyone we know?"

"Yes," Susannah replied before either of the two detectives could respond.

"Who?" Craig turned to her with eyebrows knit into question marks.

"Mr. Russo," Detective Lyons cleared his throat. "Did you know a Jake Winthrop?"

"Jake. Jake . . ." Craig paused. "Yes," he sighed, "I'm afraid I do."

Detective Fields stepped aside to reveal half a dozen photographs on the table of what appeared to be a corpse. Their yearbook was opened to a group picture of the football team and individual photographs of the players. Fields picked up one of the photos and held it before Craig at eye level.

"Remember him?" Fields's eyes stared over the photograph.

Craig winced as he took the picture of a half-naked mutilated corpse from the detective. The contorted body lay amid a patch of blood-soaked grass. The right forearm had been severed at the elbow, and the left leg was positioned in an L facing to the outside. A pile of what appeared to be intestines slithered down the right side of the midsection from a cavernous gash that began at the sternum and ended just below the belly button; one long strand of intestine lay zigzagged on the grass and stretched just below the feet of the body. The face a bloody piñata.

"Um, christ." Craig took a seat; the laceration on his forehead began to throb. "My goodness. Are you sure this is Jake? I mean, this body looks like it was attacked by a shark."

"Unfortunately," Lyons began, "it's not that easy. Sharks don't attack people on land." He grinned. "Besides, we found his wallet and jewelry nearby, all of which have been identified by his girlfriend and next of kin. That rules out robbery. Furthermore," Lyons scratched his chin, "fingerprints and dental records are a 100 percent match. The body, or rather, what's left of if, fits the description given to us by witnesses present at the high school reunion."

Susannah sat down next to Craig and squeezed his hand while avoiding the pictures.

Craig placed the picture on the table and picked up another of a face so badly shredded that were it not for the teeth could have easily been mistaken for a Rorschach. The lower jaw had been dislocated to produce a sinister smile. He laid the picture back on the table with care.

Susannah got up and offered the men coffee. Lyons declined, Fields accepted.

"Mr. Russo, we understand that you started a fight with Jake this past Friday at your high school reunion, is that correct?" Lyons arranged the photographs neatly in two rows facing toward Craig. "A fight in which you received that injury on your forehead." He nodded at Craig's wound. "You must've been pretty upset that night."

"I'd hardly call it a fight." The throbbing of the wound intensified. He ran his fingers gingerly over the bump and chuckled. "Is that what you were told?" He shook his head. "You got this all wrong. I didn't start any fight."

"But you sure ended it." Fields narrowed his eyes and smirked.

"No." Craig pointed at the pictures. "I didn't do this if that's what you're insinuating." He returned Fields's stare. "We were involved in a slight altercation, and yes, the guy is, was, a grade A asshole, but never in a million years would I have been angry enough to do something like this." He thrust an angry index finger at the pictures.

Susannah returned with the coffee just in time to catch Craig's last remarks.

"Where did you go after the party?" Fields sipped his coffee.

"Home." Craig rolled his eyes. "We came home."

"What time was it? Do you remember?" Fields continued.

"About eleven something." Susannah jumped in. "It was almost twelve. I brought him straight home. We have witnesses who saw us get into the car and leave. I can give you the names if it'll help."

"That would be helpful," Lyons replied in a monotone.

She pulled out her cellular phone and gave them the names and phone numbers of Sally and the other girls.

Fields fixed his eyes on Craig while his partner wrote. Craig was compelled to look away under the weight of Fields's iron stare.

"Thank you very much." Lyons smiled as he finished jotting down the last name.

"Listen, detectives, I've had a hell of a weekend and up until now was having somewhat of a good day, so let's cut all the bullshit and tell me exactly what I am being accused of." He held up a stiff hand as the anger swelled within him. "No. Wait. Let me guess. According to your elaborate investigative work, you found out that Jake and I had a fight on

Friday during our high school reunion in which I received a pummeling after being embarrassed and was so furious that I decided to exact revenge by ripping his arm off, tearing open his stomach, and playing jump rope with his intestines, and for the exclamation point, lay into his face with a chainsaw." He leaned forward. "Did I miss anything?"

"Mr. Russo," Fields placed the empty cup on the table. "We're not here to accuse you of anything, but you do understand that we have to interview every person acquainted with the victim especially those that were present that night. We have to examine every possible angle and try to establish a connection—"

"You mean motive," Craig interrupted.

"Something like that." Lyons leaned forward and clasped his hands.

"And since I had a fight with Jake this past Friday night you'd figured that I was out to settle the score, out for revenge." Craig leaned back and sighed. He placed a hand on his brow. "This sucks."

For the next hour, Craig was practically forced to provide a detailed account of his dealings with Jake throughout high school: how Jake picked on "his kind," how Jake got his kicks giving wedgies during gym, how Jake once pounded a friend of his who covered up his answer sheet while Jake was trying to stare, and a couple of other discomforting mementos. He even told them about the nickname Helmethead with which Jake had branded him. The reemergence of the memories plunged Craig back into his high school years. Everything he had built and struggled to forget, all the fond memories and lovemaking with Susannah had been reduced to cinders as he concluded that she had somehow settled for second best, perhaps even third. He viewed himself as a charity case, a social experiment. Even the detectives before him exuded a level of confidence and manliness that had eluded him throughout his entire life.

"And you hadn't seen him since high school, is that correct?" Lyons added.

Craig nodded robotically.

"And you, Mrs. Russo," Fields looked at Susannah. "Have you had any contact with the victim since high school? Any contact at all?"

A knot formed and tightened in Craig's stomach.

"No," she responded, staring at Fields before turning to Craig. "None at all. I had not seen him until this past Friday night," she confessed to Craig. "The rest is as my husband told you. Nothing else." Her attempt at a smile turned into a painful smirk.

"Well then, I guess we're done." Fields gathered up the photographs and straightened them on the table before placing them in a manila envelope.

AL BRUNO

Lyons got up and straightened his tie. He reached into his coat pocket and pulled out a bundle of business cards rolled with a rubber band. He peeled one out and extended it to Craig who simply stared at it.

"Thank you." Susannah grabbed the card.

"Call us if you hear anything or remember something that you may have not included in your statement. People sometimes recall little details days after an accident," Lyons stated.

Fields thanked her for the coffee. She stepped out with the two detectives for several minutes before coming in and closing the door gently. She sat down next to Craig and grabbed his hand; he pulled it away.

"What's wrong?" She drew closer.

Craig looked away.

"Hey." She rubbed his knee. "Craig, talk to me."

"Why did you marry me?"

"Huh?"

"You could've had any jock in school, yet you settled for me." He paused. "Why?"

"Why on earth are you asking me a question like that? I love you." She reached for his hand and grabbed it forcefully. "I love you."

"Then why did you have to tell him about how Jake harassed me in school?" He reached for the yearbook.

"Honey, I . . ." Her eyes swelled with tears. "Please. They knew about the high school reunion, so I figured I'd show them the yearbook." She began to cry. "I didn't know. I didn't mean anything by it." She released his hand and hugged herself. "I'm sorry."

Craig got up and sent the yearbook flying across the room; it landed at the base of the fireplace.

"Not only have you officially made me a suspect, but more importantly, you've finally managed to remind me of where I stand in your little world." He walked to the window.

"You were with me. We have witnesses."

"Suzy," Craig turned around furiously. "You're my wife. Of course, you're supposed to back up my story. They know that. They also know, *after you told them*, that we came home and got drunk. As if that wasn't enough, you also mentioned that you passed out before me. This means, as the prosecutor might argue, at which point I may have gone out and murdered Jake and had enough time to wash away the evidence before you woke up."

"But . . . but . . . you were with me." Her voice trailed off.

"How do you know?" Craig raised his hands. "You were out cold."

"You're starting to scare me." Susannah wiped away her tears.

"Don't you understand?" He ran a nervous hand through his hair. "I have a weak alibi. There is a time gap that is unaccounted for and which you cannot back up because you were passed out."

"You're innocent. You were home with me."

"Was I?" He chuckled. "After all, isn't it a coincidence that Jake's body turns up hours after he and I get into it?" He leaned against the windowsill. "Perhaps if you would have listened to me I wouldn't be in this mess." He shook his head. "We should have never gone to that damn reunion!"

Susannah placed a hand over her mouth and ran into the bedroom. She slammed the door and threw herself on the bed. Her cries reached Craig's ears.

"Dammit!" he cursed through his teeth and brought a fist down on the windowsill.

Craig escaped to the back porch with a six-pack to ease his pain and a cigar in celebration of Jake's death; there was no guilt. Once the six-pack was gone, he went in to check on Susannah who had fallen asleep in a fetal position with a pillow held tightly against her chest: her snores the result of the toll that anguish and fatigue had taken on her over the past several days. He kissed her on the forehead and left the room, grabbed some more beers, and went back out, staring at the trees while enjoying the breeze and what remained of the sunset. There was no interest in working on his car. He just sat back and enjoyed his beer.

10:46 p.m.

He had fallen into a siesta and awoke to the porch and driveway lights turning on and off. The floodlights and motion sensors had gone up several years ago after Susannah claimed to have felt "someone" or "some *thing*" watching her at night. On several occasions, she had awakened in the middle of the night to a dreadful feeling that there was a presence outside and even swore that she had seen a shadow in the patio while getting a glass of water.

"I think there's somebody outside." She shook him vigorously. "Craig, Craig."

Craig sat up like a zombie smacking his gums and sauntered groggily to the living room, dragging an aluminum bat like a caveman, slid open the patio door, and stepped onto the porch like a half-drunk pinch hitter.

"Be careful, honey." She followed three paces behind with a twelve-inch chef's knife.

"Would you put that away before you hurt yourself. Or worse, me." He scanned the yard. "There's nothing out here."

"Well, I thought I heard something."

"We're at the base of the woods, Suzy. There's always going to be some type of strange noise." He walked back in while taking the knife. "We are not alone." He yawned. "I'm going to bed."

She had remained on the porch caressing her arms. Her eyes pierced the darkness as the feeling of being watched came back. This time, however, she did not waiver. There was something recognizable in the air, a filial bond with the night. Seconds later, she went back inside and locked the door.

From across the yard, behind the fence, Athena stared back.

Craig yawned and checked his watch. Three hours had elapsed. After checking on Susannah who was still fast asleep, he washed his face and grabbed a bottle of whiskey from the bar. He used his shirt tail to brush off the thin layer of dust on the bottle. *Ah, what the hell. I'll call in tomorrow. I got a shitload of days coming to me anyway.* He took a couple of swigs before deciding to visit his daughter.

He thought about Jake's folly as he walked deeper into the woods. Although there was a sense of humanitarian pity, he was mostly relieved and reprimanded himself for relishing in the death of another human being. But if anybody deserved it, it was Jake. *Besides, it wasn't me that killed him. Just one less asshole in the world.*

Craig reached the clearing, splashed into the stream, and stumbled several feet. He took another swig and brought a cupped hand to his mouth.

"Athena!" He blew kisses into the air. "Daddy's here." He motioned with his hands; the bottle swung back and forth like a pendulum. "Come on, baby. Daddy needs a hug." He lowered his voice and brought the bottle to his lips. "Boy, does daddy need a hug today."

There was a ruffling in the branches overhead followed by grunting and panting. A dark silhouette descended the tree like an ape. Ten feet from the ground, the creature pushed itself from the tree and landed on all fours with a loud thud. It stood upright for a couple of seconds before dropping back down to all fours and running to Craig.

"Hey, baby." He smiled. "How's Daddy's little girl tonight?"

Athena slowed down, stood upright, and walked toward Craig. He put his arms around her powerful body and came to rest on the bony ridges protruding from her spine. He hugged his daughter; she hugged him harder.

"Agh!" He patted her back. "Okay, okay. Daddy loves you too." He reached for her arms. "You can let go now."

She let go of the vice grip and ran around in circles occasionally rolling on the ground.

"Aren't you the happy one tonight." Craig nearly fell backward as he cocked his head for another drink. "What are you so happy about?"

Athena ran back and forth playfully. Craig tried to restrain her but gave up after she knocked him to the ground from the excitement. He sat up and brushed the dirt from the neck of his bottle and laughed.

"Hey, guess what? Guess who got whacked this weekend?" He drank and cleared his throat. "Come on, I'll give you one guess." He held up an index finger.

Athena walked leisurely toward Craig. Her eyes seemed overly bright, even menacing, causing him to blink momentarily. She had the same predatory look a couple of days ago.

"Athena?" Craig swallowed hard.

"J . . . a . . . k . . . e . . ." She crept closer.

"What?" He frowned.

"J . . . a . . . k . . . e . . ."

The hairs on the back of Craig's neck sprang to attention. His chest tightened as Athena drew closer with a devilish grin, a ghastly array of jagged teeth accompanied by predatory eyes highlighted by the moonlight. He tried to scamper backward but was unable to move. She grabbed his right hand and pulled it to her effortlessly. He did not resist.

"D . . a . . d . . . d . . . eee . . . D . . . a . . . d . . . d . . . eeee," she grunted and held a closed fist in her right hand over Craig's hand.

"Yes, I'm Daddy." Tears of joyful fear streamed down his face. His smile quivered as he dropped to his knees.

"Da . . . dee." Her voice was raspy. "J . . . a . . . k . . . e." Athena opened her hand and placed two small spheres in the palm of his hand.

"Baby?" Craig weighed the rubbery objects in his hand, the pounding in his chest unbearable. "What is this?"

Athena gazed at him in malevolent silence.

AL BRUNO

Moonlight fell on the two spheres as he brought them to eye level. Craig stared into a pair of eyes. The bottle of whiskey fell and keeled over, spilling what remained into the earth.

"Oh, my . . ." Craig looked up at his daughter's powerful silhouette. The broad shoulders swayed lightly as she clicked her talons all together. Her eyes absorbed the brightness of the moon as they cut through the veil of night from side to side. Her legs were slightly bent as if ready to spring. She seemed darker than the surrounding forest.

"Jake." Athena's words were now recognizable.

Craig squeezed the orbs in his hands as a smile broke across his face.

"I love you . . ." He wept.

THE LOST DAUGHTER

What a beautiful mother, and yet more beautiful daughter!

—Horace (65-8 BC)

August 5, 2009, 7:00 a.m.

I F THERE EXISTS a realm solely for hysteria, Craig was ruler. If euphoria could manifest itself into a physical entity, Craig had embraced it. If delirium was a disease, Craig was both carrier and plague.

He had returned home just before dawn in a state of extreme nirvana, floating from the jubilant night spent with Athena, kicking twigs and whistling, sometimes humming. This morning's air was different, purer, lighter, intoxicating. He felt as if he had learned to breathe once again; the lungs had been refurbished, and a placid aura had engulfed his soul. After years of torment, there was finally peace in his heart.

Susannah stirred and opened her eyes. The bright green numbers on the clock read 7:01 a.m. The noise on the patio door sliding open followed by heavy footsteps and humming had jarred her from her sleep. *One thing is for sure, with all the ruckus, it is definitely not a thief.* She sat up and rubbed her eyes. Yesterday's argument lingered in her mind as she massaged her temples in circles to no avail. *Excedrin and coffee should do the trick.*

She opened the bedroom door and stepped out; the patio door was half open. She closed it and called to her husband; there was no response. Dirt footprints led into the guest bedroom. Pausing momentarily to look at the clock, she went to the door and knocked gently.

"Craig? Are you in there?"

No response.

"Craig?" She opened the door and poked her head inside.

He lay splattered on the bed like a bug on a windshield, shirt and pants soiled in dirt and dress shoes caked with mud.

"Craig." She approached him and was about to nudge him when a bellowing snore followed by farting caused her to flinch. He smacked his gums and turned to his side: more snoring and farting.

"Guess who's not going to work today?" She crossed her arms then proceeded to undress him, taking off his shoes, scooping up some of the mud that had fallen on the floor in her hands. "Where in the world have you been?" She leaned over and kissed him on the cheek. "Whew!" She covered her nose and swatted the air while throwing a quilt over him. "You smell like a dog."

"I love you," she uttered softly and exited the room.

5:47 p.m.

Beep! Beep! Beep! Susannah opened the microwave door and took out the cup of hot water. She shook a bag of instant coffee before tearing it open and pouring it into the cup, staring at the whirlpool inside as she stirred. Through the corner of her eye, she spotted the yearbook peeking from underneath the sofa where Craig had flung it yesterday and looked away while holding back tears.

She opened the patio door and stepped onto the porch, closing her eyes and inhaling the fragrant scent of pine as a sudden gust of wind welcomed her, running its gentle fingers through her hair. The sun had begun its daily repose, giving way to the nocturnal luminous orb in the sky. Effervescent hues of blue and purple draped themselves over shades of orange and yellow in giant brush strokes.

So much confusion, so much pain. Her life with Craig had been nothing short of a dream, and if there ever was a mold for an ideal man, he had been cast from it. Every day with him was like the first day for them. He would always hug and kiss her before leaving for work and embrace her when he returned. He never complained about anything and was always surprising her with little gifts and spontaneous ideas like the time she came home from work to a candlelight dinner in the backyard with tiki torches. She smiled at the memory while sipping her coffee. She couldn't even remember when was the last time they had argued. There was practically nothing to complain about, almost nothing.

The fact that she was unable to get pregnant was the only stigma to their otherwise ideal marriage. They had spent thousands of dollars and dozens of hours in clinics trying various methods of fertilization without any success. Until they came across Dr. Barnaby Spencer, who had brought hope into their life by announcing the release of Fertilisure, a drug capable of boosting fertilization by up to 75 percent, a drug that he had assisted in creating in collaboration with three other doctors and two scientists. Although the drug—which was administered by pills a week after menstruation—proved promising in laboratory experiments, it was still fairly new in the market. "Women who have taken it," Barnaby had commented, "have had better than average results." *But,* Susan thought at the time, *was this fertilization drug nothing but a placebo?* It had appeared so to the FDA who pulled it from the shelves within a year after dozens of incidents of miscarriages, stillborns, and deformed children from women who had been subjected to the drug flooded the news. Barnaby had come to them as an angel but turned out to be a serpent. They had lost contact with him months after her first and only trip to the delivery room; he had resigned his practice due to increasing lawsuits and the constant harassing from local newshounds who had set up tents outside his office and home.

After the nightmare in the delivery room, they consulted an Oriental infertility specialist who recommended an organic solution to their dilemma. Craig had immediately taken a liking to the little Chinese man who spoke in parables and constantly pushed his glasses up his nose as he shuffled back and forth retrieving pamphlets of all sorts for his guests. Despite the colorful brochures and show-and-tell presentation by the enthusiastic caricature as he displayed an assortment of plants and herbs that he kept in a small refrigerator, Susannah had remained indifferent throughout the entire visitation. Craig, on the other hand, smiled and nodded every time the old man dangled some leaves in front of him. An hour and $175 later, they walked out of the office; Craig even bowed to the old man upon leaving. He read the prescription of plants and herbs the old man had given him and beamed.

"I got a good feeling about this." He waved the piece of paper.

"We'll see." Susannah managed a counterfeit smile.

They drove straight to the store listed on the back of the prescription; the drive lasted over thirty minutes.

"Is that Webster Avenue?" He pointed at the hieroglyphics. "Is this an *L* or a *T*?"

"That's an *L*. It's Wesley Avenue."

Craig continued another mile before making a right on Wesley Avenue, where the border between American society ended and Chinese began. Signs bore the names of stores in large bold Chinese characters on top and their English translation just below. Every street had just about an equal number of street vendors to stores. Parades of people spilled onto the streets as there was barely enough room on the sidewalks. Susannah kept repeating for Craig to slow down as she pointed at pedestrians who seemed oblivious to traffic. Storefronts were beautifully decorated in a cornucopia of colors. Dragons of various sizes, shapes, and colors stared from the stores at the couple as they drove by. One dragon in particular caught Susannah's eye: thick scales in emerald green with a silver underbelly; a golden sail decorated with a collage of symbols and mythical characters engaging in battle began at the top of the skull and gradually grew as it descended down its back, tapering at the tail; and a powerful snout with menacing teeth complimented with a bright-red forked tongue that slithered from in between the two lower fangs. A pair of onyx eyes kept vigil on the couple as they pulled in front of the store.

Susannah rubbed her arms while Craig matched the numbers on the paper with the numbers on the store.

"We're here." He smiled and patted Susannah's knee.

Susannah locked stares with the dragon as she stepped out of the car, fighting the feeling of being mocked by the reptilian sentinel.

"Okay." Craig rubbed his hands together.

"Hardly looks like a pharmacy."

"It's Oriental, you know." Craig shrugged. "It's different. But"—he smiled and thumbed at the door—"in there lies the cure."

"I didn't know I was sick." Susannah looked away.

"Honey, I . . . I didn't mean it like that. You know that. I . . ." He took a deep breath. "Listen, I admit it doesn't look like much, but it's an option. The least we can do is give it a try."

Susannah looked around: the dragons on the other side had sealed off the entire street; the people had metamorphosed into one giant impregnable wall of flesh—there was no way out except through the store. She closed her eyes and took a deep breath before pushing past Craig and stopping at the door. "Let's get this over with."

Ten months into the treatment, she called it quits. She had been taking a mixture of dried and powdered banyan roots with milk after each menstrual cycle for over six months without any results. Craig argued that she give it another two months; she declined.

"How about the tea with Jamun leaves and honey the doctor recommended?"

"I've devoured an entire forest, and so far, nothing." Susannah flailed her arms. "If I eat one more damn leaf, I swear I'll be able to carry out photosynthesis." She shook her head in defeat. "I'm sorry. I can't do this anymore."

"But we have to keep trying," he would respond with desperation in his eyes.

"Yes, I know, but let it happen naturally. Not because of some stupid drug or silly drink from a plant. When God wants us to have a child, he'll send us one."

A tear fell in her coffee. She wiped her face and threw the remainder of the coffee on the grass. Her hands went to her belly.

"Oh god, when?"

6:18 p.m.

Bam! Bam! Bam!

Two sledgehammers slammed against the side of his temples from the inside. Two veins pulsed at his sides like a pair of water hoses about to explode. He clutched the sides of his head. An attempt to sit up resulted in a sudden spinning of the room that brought his cranium to the brink of eruption. He leaned back and closed his eyes; the wooziness was accompanied by extreme thirst and coughing.

"Suzy," he cried weakly. The clock read 6:18 p.m. *Shit. I've been out all day.* He sat up slowly and placed his head between his hands.

"Suzy," he called, this time a bit louder. *Dammit. Where is she?*

He got up, took two steps, and bolstered himself against the wall. He opened the door and shuffled into the living room like a newborn zombie. The furniture seemed to have moved, or had it always been like this? Something had collided with his foot. He looked down and saw the yearbook, the primary source of all the recent misery. Craig clutched the sofa as he kneeled to pick it up; his vision blurred. His legs buckled, and he came to rest on the floor with the yearbook clutched to his chest.

He sat up and looked around; the patio door was wide open. He carefully grabbed onto the back of the sofa and dragged himself up, tossing the yearbook on the cushions. The haze in his head steadied, but the pounding continued. In the kitchen, he grabbed a bottle of water and gulped it with the vigor of a triathlete after a ten-mile race, erasing the dryness in his throat. He ran a hand across his mouth, searched for another bottle, and made his way to the medicine cabinet in search of aspirin.

The sun had completely disappeared. Stars began to appear one by one like speckles from a cosmic paintbrush. And as the blue and purple hues slowly disintegrated on the horizon, the ebony backdrop of the universe draped itself across the sky like a huge tablecloth. Within minutes, the night had reclaimed its designated part of the day.

Susannah hugged herself as she gazed at the stars. Their serenity called to her; the gentle breath of the forest calmed her mind and soul.

"Suzy?" Craig stepped onto the porch kneading his temples. "Hey, what are you doing?"

"Nothing." She took a deep breath. "Just thinking."

"About?"

"Nothing and everything." She shrugged, turned to him, and ran a hand across his cheek. "Sleep well?"

"Yeah," he nodded. "Didn't know it was this late."

"Don't worry. I called Paul this morning and told him you had woken up with a sore back and that you'd be in tomorrow." She smiled and placed her head on his chest.

"Thanks."

"Craig, I'm sorry about yesterday. I shouldn't have done that."

"It's okay." He stroked her hair.

"And I'm sorry about making you go to the reunion."

"It's not your fault. Nobody could have foreseen what was going to happen. That asshole definitely had it coming to him." He paused and stared into the forest. "Sometimes, things just happen. And you have to accept them no matter how . . . ugly they are."

"I know." She wiped her face and turned around. But it's just—"

"Hey. Don't worry about it. We're going to be okay."

She began to sob silently.

"Suzy, what's wrong?"

"Oh Craig." She buried her face in her hands. "I'm so sorry."

"I said it was okay." He grabbed her by the shoulders. "Don't worry about it."

"Not about that." She shook her head.

"Then what is it?"

She took a deep breath and stared at him. "A baby."

"Huh?"

"I know how much you have been longing for a child even though you don't bring it up. And I haven't been able to give you one." Tears sped down her face.

It was Craig's turn to take a deep breath.

"We've tried everything," she continued, "but nothing has worked. It's all my fault."

"Listen, stop it." He wiped her tears with his thumbs. "I love you. No matter what, I love you."

"But I wanted to give you kids. I wanted a family." She gestured to their yard. "I wanted to fill this place up with kids. At least one. That's all I ask for, just one."

Craig smiled. *And you have.*

"So many times have I stood here and prayed for a child." She shook her head in defeat. "Nothing."

His heart beat faster as a wave of joy crashed into him. The time had finally come. He pushed away from her and hurried inside.

"Where are you going?"

"Just a second," he yelled over his shoulder.

"Craig, you haven't heard a word I've said," she whispered, feeling as if a priest had gotten tired of her confession.

He emerged with a huge childish grin.

"What's that for? And that?" She pointed at his hands.

"This is for navigating." He waved the flashlight. "And this," he waved a bottle of champagne, "is for celebrating."

"Have you lost your mind?"

"No, I haven't." He walked past her toward the back gate. "Come on." He waved her over.

"Craig, stop. What are you doing?"

"Will you just come?" He unlatched the gate.

"Where to?" She crossed her arms.

"Come. Follow me."

"One minute, we're having a serious discussion, and the next, you want to go out to the woods and drink champagne? You're scaring me."

"Suzy," his voice dropped as his eyes bore deep into hers. "There's nothing to be scared of. Trust me." He stared at the woods. "Nothing in there will harm us."

"Are you feeling okay?" She walked to him.

"Do you love me?" He turned to her with a look toeing the line of insanity.

She stared at him for several seconds. "Yes."

"Do you trust me?"

"Yes." She crossed her arms and sighed.

"Then let's go." He grabbed her hand gently. "There's somebody I'd like you to meet."

"In there?!" She pointed at the woods.

He nodded.

"Craig?" The hairs on her neck hopped to attention.

"It's okay." He pulled her gently into the woods. "I want you to meet your daughter."

She felt herself floating as he pulled her along. Her mind submerged itself into a maelstrom of dreadful mysticism as they entered the womb of the forest.